Reading the Coffee Grounds
and
Other Stories

by

Niles Reddick

Aakenbaaken & Kent

Aakenbaaken & Kent

Reading the Coffee Grounds and Other Stories

Aakenbaaken & Kent
aakenbaakeneditor@gmail.com

Cover design by David Skinner

ISBN: 978-1-938436-50-5

For Audrey and Nicholas

Table of Contents

The Last Word

When she turned seventy, Annis spent what had been writing time taking care of her husband: preparing breakfast, dishing out a handful of pills for everything from acid reflux to anti-stroke, cleaning the wheelchair with alcohol wipes, changing his diaper and wiping his privates, sponging him with soap and water, and spoon feeding him. Home health from the state came twice a week, but these tasks had to be done daily. Since high school, they'd done everything together from working the farm to raising their children and taking care of and later burying their parents. Somewhere in between, Annis had managed to write, mostly in the morning, reading everything out loud to him and catching her own grammatical and content errors.

She had her first publications in small literary magazines, managed by artsy folks who loved her Faulkneresque style, her keen Weltyish description, her O-Connor-like wit, yet what she wielded on the keyboard was different and unfolded in its own distinct Southern style. Set in a geographic region of swampland South with rough, God-loving characters who straddled the thin line between saved and sin, her ten novels, two collections of stories, and countless other stories raised eyebrows. Through the years, Annis had anorexic literary agents who wore all black, old gay giants of publishers who were known to make starving artist discoveries, and media hounds who pounced on every new story.

Annis didn't travel much at all because of anxiety and previous wrecks, the last of which was the most traumatic. She'd been plotting and describing her story, "Julie's Song", a modern version of a Shakespearean love story with rape and spousal abuse by a grotesque figure when she'd hit a pine log truck head on. Though the air bag saved her, she had been jolted back to reality and came to the conclusion she could no longer drive because she was so obsessed with stories. So, Waylon had driven and she told him stories and he offered his opinion and enjoyed watching her on stage speak to crowds who smothered Annis afterward for a signature while Waylon dreamed of book royalties turning into a new John Deere combine with an air conditioned cab with a FM stereo, but when Annis found Waylon slumped at the breakfast table, blood running from his nose, muttering gibberish and not able to lift his right side, she knew they'd scale back readings and book signings and farming, promoting books on social media and renting the land to keep income flowing to pay for health care.

As the weeks passed, the agent moved on to clients churning out youth fiction and chic lit, the publisher rejected the eleventh based on falling sales on paperbacks, gigs dried up, and the media covered book fairs in larger cities where they picked what writers they thought would appeal most, like apples in a tree. Annis knew she would and could focus on Waylon and plot and transcribe when he slept and at night when the moon shone light through the kitchen window and the owls called to each other, but most of all Annis knew that as the crowds faded, she would save the best for last and would have the last word, a word people read and talked about long after the other movie goers had gone home.

The Ministry

When we got the call that my wife's grandmother had passed away at ninety-two, we weren't really surprised because once one gets into her nineties there's only so much time left. Of course, in our twenty years of marriage, we had been told each year by my wife's mother that we should come visit because "this is probably her last year." Fortunately, and as usual, her mother was wrong, and her grandmother lived relatively well until a sudden internal bleed took her quickly, though we were unclear if she died on Sunday or Monday, not that it really mattered. What we needed to know for planning purposes was when the visitation and funeral were to be held, so we could rearrange life: work schedules, church, piano lessons for our daughter, taekwondo for both children.

Though we hadn't seen her often through the years given that she lived several hours distance from us, my wife loved her grandmother, and I always thought highly of her as well. She was always positive to us and wrote lengthy messages in cards about how proud she was of us, of our children, of our lives. Her script was in cursive, a form of writing no longer taught in schools, and seemed to indicate serious tremors in her hand. I imagined it would take her hours to get a card out to one of her children, grandchildren, great-grandchildren, nearly forty all combined. She often included Bible verses, too, an idea she had given a great deal of thought and what she imagined might be fitting given what she knew of the family member. That was her ministry. My guess is that she sent hundreds of cards a year, helping a struggling postal service. Given that her generation is dying off, and there continues to be an increase in web communication, I expect the postal service will suffer a tremendous blow in the near future.

Aside from the day and time of death, my mother-in-law had apparently told uncles, aunts, cousins, friends, and ex's (yes, I said ex's because of multiple marriages in some of the family who were still considered family given shared children and grandchildren, a phenomenon still alien in my own immediate family) that a cousin, who lived outside the town of Thomasville, Georgia, where the visitation and funeral would be held, would host everyone for a dinner. More important, she told them all that my wife and her sister-in-law would prepare the food. My mother-in-law conveniently forgot to tell my wife and her sister-in-law, but when they couldn't pull it off, my mother-in-law communicated back to her family that my wife and her sister-in-law "weren't willing to do it," making my wife and her sister-in-law look bad. Conversely, this fabrication made my mother-in-law appear to be the sweet angel who was attempting to help everyone in the family, a life-long perception she attempted to project. After all, she is a nurse, but if I was laid up, I wouldn't want her coming at me with any needle because it might be full of arsenic. I imagined her to be like a librarian I had once worked with who was rumored to have been ordering and reading books on poison shortly before her husband died of mysterious illnesses, though he had several issues. It wasn't long after, though, the librarian had a new boyfriend, but he died within the year. She followed that with another boyfriend turned husband, but she left the library and moved, so no one knows if he is still living.

Normally, I don't even answer the phone anymore, even if it's her family members or my own. I think after being on the phone at work so much, I've found it to be an annoyance in my life I can do without. I have a cell phone for emergencies and people get mad because I don't turn it on, nor do I have voicemail set-up on it. In several conversations with family members, my wife was reporting to me details one morning over coffee and said something matter-of-factly that struck me as odd: her cousin Jack was bringing the grandmother in a van.

"What the hell did you say?" I asked.

"What do you mean?" she responded.

"Did you just say your cousin was hauling your grandmother to Georgia in the back of a van?"

"I think that's what someone said," she said.

"Don't you find that odd?"

"Well, I guess so. I really didn't think about it."

"I know they live in Tennessee and all, but I don't think you can just pick up a dead person and transport them out of state. You can bet I'll find out."

At the visitation, I was itching to find a way to get to Jack and ask, particularly since we'd only met once through the years and I didn't even know him. He was outside smoking and I cornered him and said, "I appreciate all you had to do."

"Man, you wouldn't believe it," he laughed. "I didn't mind hauling her in the back of the van. You know I did it for my uncle and my grandpa, too, but I didn't expect all this."

"What do you mean?"

"Oh, you didn't hear? I picked up the box at the funeral home and signed papers."

"A box?"

"Yeah, cardboard. Probably charged us for that, too."

I was already shocked, but the next piece increased the level.

"I got to somewhere in North Georgia when Mama called and said, 'Jack, where are you? Have you left yet?' I told her, 'Yeah, mama, I'm already in North Georgia,' and she said, 'Damn, we forgot to get her clothes on and she's in the box naked.' I said, "Lord, Mama, what you want me to do about it? I ain't turning around and driving four hours back to Knoxville.' She said, 'Just go buy her a nice pink dress when you get down there. We got her a pink casket.' Man, was I floored. I've got my grandma in the back of my van and she's naked."

I smiled. "Did she sell Mary Kay?"

"I don't think so," he said. "She never wore much make-up. Ain't that crazy, though? She was in there naked. I never seen her naked and weren't about to go and look either, but it just freaked me out. I smoked a little before getting back on the road just to keep me even."

"Wow," I said. "That is some story." I wondered how odd it would have been if his marijuana- induced driving would have caused him to be pulled over by the Georgia State Patrol and had to endure a search.

"I got to the funeral home in Thomasville right after they closed, and one man was getting in his car, and I eased the van in and blocked him, got out, and told him, 'Hey man, I got my naked grandma back here in the box, and you ain't going nowhere till you get her out of my van.'"

"Well, at least someone was still there." At that point, another relative came up and started talking to Jack and I moved back inside to visit more. The rest of the visitation went well, people hugging and telling stories. One of my wife's aunts hit on me and another aunt slapped her fifth husband at the funeral because he told her to calm down. Other than that, the service was fairly uneventful and went smoothly. When we arrived back home, I checked the mail and my heart skipped a beat when underneath the weekly shopper, credit card junk mail, and business flyers lay a card addressed to my wife from her grandmother, apparently mailed the day before she died. She waited a few days to open it, and it was the same sweet grandmother, praising us, ministering to us, and offering scripture on the eve of her own departure.

The Pool

"It's $30 dollars a month," my mama said to my daddy. We knew she thought the pool membership cost too much. We pulled at Daddy's work shirt, with his name stitched on the pocket and drenched with his sweat from the Georgia heat and humidity, begging, "Please." We wanted to join the pool for the summer in the small rural town to which we'd recently moved. Our new neighbors were going and so were most of our friends from school who lived in town. Our country friends worked on their farms and couldn't. The coolness they experienced was from a hose fastened to a spigot piped to a well. "We'll see," Daddy said, shooing us to the den, where we watched the TV that picked up three channels if the antenna was straight and where we breathed bleach fumes from my Mama's having scrubbed mildew from baseboards.

The next morning, Mama gave me an envelope. "Don't you lose it. You give this to Ms. Wilma Jean. It's the signed application and check." The screen door slammed as we took off through the yard to the road on our bikes. Mama wouldn't see us again until supper. My sister had the pimento cheese sandwiches in a paper sack, and when we arrived, and laid our bikes on the grass next to others, Ms. Wilma Jean handed me a key and put the bag in a locker. She looked over the paperwork and gave us a nod. "No running," she yelled after us.

The water was cold. We got it in our ears, we swallowed it periodically, and people splashed us in our eyes by cupping hands and spraying or by jumping in and doing cannon balls or belly flops. Teenage girls sprawled on beach towels on a cement patio near the deep end and guys stood huddled by a tree gawking, flexing muscles, and talking and laughing. Once that first week, the pool got cleared because of a suspected turd that turned out to be a Baby Ruth dropped in as a joke.

By the end of summer, we were tanned and our black hair was lighter. We didn't want summer to end, but the next spring, we were excited about the pool until we learned it would not open. After school got out, we rode bikes and stood by the fence and watched a bulldozer fill it in. Our daddy told us, "They don't want everyone coming, so they'd rather close it altogether." We found other things to do in summer, and it would be years before we learned a local group had protested to the international charitable organization that owned the pool that it was unfair to sell memberships to whites only.

Visiting

In the fall of 1976, we sixth graders were thrilled our Georgia Governor Carter had been elected President of the United States and that we'd celebrated the bicentennial of our country. Our community had come together for a parade with the high school marching band, the mayor in a convertible waving, and our church youth singing the good news on a float pulled by our song director's Ford F-150. The next day, Sunday morning, our twelve-year-old group of boys marched into the sanctuary of the Baptist church, sitting near the back, so we could pass notes, send spitball through straws to girls a few rows down, fart and laugh at ourselves.

None of that behavior violated God's word, as we understood it, but I was startled when I noticed an elderly African American woman on the front row dressed in a green dress and matching hat. I elbowed James who, in turn, elbowed Mark. We were quiet and watched. It was the first time any of us had ever seen an African American in our church in the small Georgia town. The African American Baptist church was just across the railroad tracks near the butcher shop, and I wondered if the old woman had gotten confused.

Confused or not, she seemed peaceful, and I watched the elderly banker's wife elbow her husband, and he stood and walked to the preacher's chair near the pulpit. I don't know what he whispered, but the minister, who was dressed in a white suit and looked like he should be peddling fried chicken instead of salvation, stood and eased up to the woman and whispered to her. The pianist craned her neck to see while hammering the keys from page 368 in the hymnal, "Brethren We Have Met to Worship".

The elderly woman planted her cane, stood, and walked up the side aisle, through the swinging doors in the vestibule, and out the front door. I noted she handed back her bulletin to the deacon. I didn't fully understand, but I understood enough to know while we had an integrated school, we didn't have integrated churches.

As the preacher made his way back to his seat by the pulpit, he nodded at the banker, and something made me get up, go out, and see where the old lady went. I looked to the left, the road leading across the tracks to the African American Baptist church, but she was nowhere to be seen, and I looked to the right, the sidewalk that headed into town, and she wasn't there. I didn't see any cars either.

"Luke, you better get in here. They startin," said the deacon handing out bulletins.

"Where'd that old woman go?"

"Probably got in a car. Now, get on in there 'fore your mama gets after you."

"Yes sir."

That incident haunted me. Not long after, there was a fight in the church over budget items, and the church split. About half of the church membership left and for a year held services at a Masonic lodge until others questioned budget items and left, too. Joining forces, the group went back to the church, voted the preacher out, and around twenty-five percent of the families left with him. The ordeal put a strain on friendships, working relationships, and community relationships. Some became Methodists, and some never went back to church. Part of me believed the elderly woman was really an angel or maybe Jesus in disguise come to test the good Baptists and they'd failed the test without ever knowing it.

Worm Grunting

Six months of being unemployed, of getting a government check, along with the food stamps, had long since put Melvin in a depressed state. He wasn't depressed to the point of sleeping all day, not bathing, and being suicidal (though he'd had thoughts of ending it, and each time he did, he saw his two sons, now in middle school, struggling without him). Each day when the light showed a strip through the curtains that wouldn't completely close, the light seemed to align perfectly with the bridge of his nose in the bed, if he was on his back, and Melvin rolled, got up, made some coffee, and got online to go through any new jobs at Monster or CareerBuilder. The search had become the norm, the daily routine he hated, not because he believed he was better than others, though he believed in his potential to do more, but because he hated being dependent on the welfare system. His own mama, still living and barely getting by on Social Security told him, "Melvin, you paid into it all these years; it's okay to get it a while until you get back on your feet."

Melvin knew that welfare was there to help people, and he knew that sooner or later, he wouldn't need it, but it seemed to be later rather than sooner. He was behind on practically every bill, had canceled his cell phone, used minimalistic electricity (relying on natural light) and water (only showering on days when he left the apartment for filling out applications or interviewing). He no longer shaved daily and so his mirror image seemed older because the gray stubble showed. Melvin even felt his computer had turned on him at times, showing ads in the margins related to hair regrowth treatments, exercise equipment, testosterone treatments, vitality drugs, and the latest, diapers for adult men to prevent leakage. What annoyed him most were not the ads, or the fact that he was older, but that he didn't invest in these technology tracking devices. Melvin didn't beat himself up about hindsight; however, he often noted how life scenarios might have worked differently for him had he made alternate choices.

Melvin was hoping the call was about an interview. "Hello?"

"Hey, Melvin. You still looking for some work?"

"Sure am."

"My cousin down in Appalachicola needs some help. He lost a guy working for him. It don't pay a lot, but it will give you some cash until you get something you want."

"Shrimp boat?"

"Nah, worm grunting."

"You drunk?"

"I ain't drunk. I said worm grunting. Never heard of it?"

"No, I haven't."

"They drive a stob in the ground. Rub a flat iron across it. Makes a sound kind of like farting, but it causes the ground to vibrate and the worms come out of the ground. They think it's a mole digging to get them, and they come oozing out of the ground in gobs. You collect the worms and they pay $25 a bucket. You can get several buckets in a day."

"Good night, I've never heard of anything like it. Where do they do this?"

"It's in the Appalachicola forest, a place called Tate's Hell."

"Why's it called Tate's Hell?"

"I don't know really. Maybe because of all the snakes and mosquitos out there."

"Hell, I'm game. I need the money to hold me over."

Melvin drove the few miles from Sopchoppy to the entrance of Tate's Hell, where he met up with the small crew. He wore snake proof boots, held a flat iron in one hand, a bucket that contained a stob in the other, and as the crew entered the forest from the two lane path the old truck sloshed down, the sunlight faded. He felt a slight temperature decrease, but not enough to stave off the high humidity and prevent excessive sweating. Melvin got used to the process quickly and before lunch had filled three buckets. One of the guys told him, "It might be in your blood. It's in mine. It's like there's an art to it. Some got the gift. Some ain't. Looks like you might've got it."

Melvin didn't know if he had a gift or not, but he did ask how many buckets they'd fill before knocking off, and the man told they tried to get a hundred dollars apiece. The old man told him they didn't work every day. Some of them would work every other day. "They might get them enough money to buy a fifth and be out the next day," he added. Melvin felt like he might try doing this for a while until the right job came along. To him, it was honest work, and the more he thought about the sound of the flat iron rubbing the stob made him think of the Aboriginal's degeridoo instrument used to praise and thank the Earth for meeting the needs of the tribe. That night, Melvin dreamed he was a painted tribal elder dancing naked around a fire to the beats of drums and listening to the low, vibrating sounds of degeridoos being played.

The Logic of High

for Gail

While upperclassman undergraduates, Matt and Tim decided to move out of the dorm and into a new apartment complex called Woodstone just a few miles from campus. Rent was considerably higher than the dorm, but there were no visiting hours, there was an outdoor pool and jacuzzi, and the driveways wound around the buildings and through the wooded wetlands offering residents a feel of nature within the city. The apartments had khaki painted siding that blended with the natural surroundings and had stone patios and entrances. Inside, fresh beige paint, popcorn ceilings, a deck overlooking the wooded areas, and dark brown carpet were features that made college students feel somehow superior to their peers still in the dorm.

Tim was slated to graduate with a Business degree and go to work for a small distribution company located half a mile from Woodstone, and Matt was a Philosophy major with no plans for the future. Though he worked full time from 3:00 p.m. until 11:00 p.m. at Ramada Inn as an evening manager, he saw himself as an existentialist plowing his own destiny moment by moment. He agreed with Sartre that hell was other people as shown in *No Exit* and that philosophy had solidified in his consciousness after dealing with carload after carload of Northerners on their way to Disney World who complained incessantly about the roaches, the mattresses, and the gnats. In the South, no amount of Raid killed roaches, and Matt had come to accept that gnats even lived in the noses and ears of all Southerners. He used to worry about them going in his mouth when he talked and his mother had told him: "Don't worry about it, Matt. They're full of protein."

Matt was off Friday, so after class, he went to the Woodstone apartment and found Tim in his room listening to Led Zeppelin on headphones. The music was so loud that Matt could understand the lyrics. "Hey," Matt waved and Tim pulled the headphones off. "Are you off tonight?"

"Yeah."

"Are you going out?"

"Nah," Matt said. "Not sure what I'm going to do." Neither Matt nor Tim were all that social. Each had his own set of friends. Tim dated a young woman who worked as a dental hygienist and Matt wasn't dating at the moment. He occasionally went out with a girl he'd dated in high school or with a group of friends from the Philosophy Club. Sometimes, he went out with a group of people from the Ramada. Dora, one of the women who worked as a clerk at the Ramada, had been dating a younger fellow and said she might come by and introduce him to Matt. Matt liked Dora. She was twenty years his senior. She was shaped like a diamond with a small head and pencil legs, but wide in the hips; she had an infectious and flirty laugh, and her long platinum frizzed hair had thinned just a tad in her early forties. She told Matt she used to iron her hair in high school to make it straight. Matt enjoyed hearing her stories about the sixties. She'd participated in marches and sit-ins, something he had never heard about from his parents.

Matt didn't remember much about the sixties, but in most of his childhood pictures, he sported a peace sign with his fingers and wore a MIA bracelet for one of his elementary teachers whose pilot husband had been shot down in Viet Nam. Matt actually fantasized about Ms. McMillian's husband never returning so he could grow up and marry his teacher, but like most fantasies of young boys, it faded the next year in fifth grade when he met Suzi. Matt told Tim Dora and her newest might stop by, so he had planned to stay around that evening, maybe order a pizza and watch a movie. Tim agreed with the idea, so they went ahead and ordered a pizza, and drove just down the road to the Castle Park shopping center to rent a couple of newer movies on VHS tapes from Blockbuster. After spending a few minutes skimming movie covers, Matt and Tim agreed on *Top Gun* and *Highlander,* two very different movies; both had been popular new rentals. While out, they stopped by the market and picked up a six-pack of Michelob. Shortly after they returned, the pizzas were delivered, the cardboard boxes so hot that steam rose when opened. First, they popped *Top Gun* in the VCR, and settled in the leather chairs in front of the TV. Nearing the end of the film, the phone rang and it was Dora, seeing if it was okay to stop by.

When the doorbell rang, Matt opened the door, said hello to Dora and shook Frank's hand. Frank didn't have a firm shake, which raised a flag. He also wore thick glasses. He was somewhat younger than

Dora and worked at a boat factory as a laborer. Flag two for Matt was when Frank tried to appear hip and talk philosophy. Matt knew he hadn't read anything. There was still some pizza left, so Frank had a piece and some beer, but Dora waived the offer away: "I have to watch my figure, darlings."

Matt invited Frank and Dora to stay and watch *Highlander*, but they giggled like children and said they were going to enjoy a romantic evening. Dora asked them if they'd like to smoke a little, and once they'd all exchanged a couple of joints between them, Matt told them he felt like his head was a balloon floating upward and away from my body. The high seemed even more powerful to Matt than the first one he had his freshman year. Everyone stared at each other and Dora's eyes seemed like glass. Matt asked them all what they thought of the origins of the universe and they all laughed, but Matt told them he had swirling images of a beginning that unfolded and expanded, like a horn of plenty at Thanksgiving. Matt also told them he could see mathematical formulas flowing onto his mind's eye and he jotted them down on a napkin. He said the formulas were unusual to him, particularly since he hadn't passed college algebra. Everyone laughed, and Dora got up from the table, tugging Frank's shirt.

"We simply must get going," Dora said. "I'll leave it up to you, Matt, darling, to solve the riddles of the universe. I have other plans."

Frank smiled, shook Matt and Tim's hands, and they were out the door.

About forty-five minutes into *Highlander*, Matt paused the VCR and answered the phone; it was Dora's teenaged daughter, Amy.

"Matt, I need your help."

"Sure, what is it?"

"Is my mom there?"

"No, she and Frank were here an hour or so ago, but they left to go back to his house."

"Something's wrong."

"What?"

"I had a dream Frank was a killer and was going to hurt mom."

"There was something strange about him."

"He lives not far from your apartment on Myrtle St. Can you go get mom and bring her home?"

"Yes, Tim and I will go."

When Matt hung up the phone, he explained the logic to Tim.

"Matt, you're high. That guy's not a killer."

"You know what? If he isn't, fine, but if he is, we can stop him. Get your shotgun."

"You have got to be kidding."

"I'm not kidding, Tim. Get the damned gun. We may have to shoot him if he has a gun."

"Oh brother. Remind me never to smoke with you again."

"I'm as clear and logical as ever, Tim."

"Whatever."

Matt and Tim went out the door. Frank's Jim Walter home was about half a mile from Woodstone, and they pulled into the sand ruts of the driveway. There were no lights on, and Tim eased his Cutlass behind Frank's VW Bug. Matt and Tim walked through the back yard to the back screened door and knocked. Matt held the gun. "Come on out here, Frank. Dora, are you okay?"

"Reckon he's already killed her or tied her up to torture her, Tim?"

"Matt, they're probably having sex."

A light in the kitchen came on; a metal pan fell on the linoleum floor followed. The back door squeaked open and the porch light came on. "Matt?"

"Dora, are you okay?"

"Yes, I'm fine," she said, stepping out onto the porch in a silk bathrobe. Frank stepped out on the porch in boxers and a t-shirt. "Matt, do you have a gun?"

"Yes, Amy called and had a bad dream that Frank was going to kill you, so I came to save you in case he was."

"I think you need to stick to your damned philosophy, Matt. Put that damned gun away," Frank said. Tim took the gun and put it in the backseat of the car.

"Go home now, Matt. I'll call Amy," Dora said. She turned and walked inside and Frank closed the door and turned off the porch light.

"Matt, you had me almost convinced something was wrong."

Matt laughed. "Well, it seemed so logical to me."

"Not really," Tim said.

Matt and Tim backtracked to Woodstone, hoping they didn't get pulled over by the police.

When Matt got to the Ramada on Monday to relieve Dora for his evening shift, she laughed. "What in the hell were you thinking?"

"It seemed logical to me at the time. What did Frank think?"

"He thought you were crazy as hell with the shotgun. We probably won't go out again."

"I'm sorry, Dora."

"No, Matt. I didn't really like him that much and I appreciate your worrying about me and coming to my rescue." Dora stood on the tip of her toes and kissed Matt on the cheek. "I wish you were older or I was younger."

Matt blushed and said thanks.

"Stick to alcohol, Matt," Dora said. "See you tomorrow."

Little Man

My son Bennett pulls only the toy vehicles that have doors that open from the rack at the grocery story because he needs one that his little man will fit. He pushes them around the house, over the granite countertops in the kitchen, the Oriental rug by the fireplace in the keeping room, across the wooden floors in the den and over the grand piano. They are chasing each other, having wrecks and having confrontations, and it reminds me of my own Matchbox collection that is probably on someone's shelf in an antique store. I wished I would've kept them and passed them to Bennett---would've saved me money.

When we get home, Bennett says the little man won't fit in the truck and he needs to go back to the grocery store and get a different one. "Not today," I said. "Next time we go, we'll exchange it."

"The little man said today," Bennett fired back.

"I don't care what the little man said." Bennett stomps up the wooden stairs to his room, and I remember the alcoholic I admitted to the detox unit at the hospital several years ago who'd seen a little man.

The sheriff's department had brought him to the hospital, and I'd processed his admissions paperwork. Because he was to be admitted to the detox unit, we'd been required to get him to voluntarily commit himself. He was young, just a few days past his nineteenth, shoulder length blonde hair, tanned. He could've passed for healthy. His family had called the sheriff after he'd shot up the house, chasing a little man.

"Can you tell me what happened?"

"Damned little man kept pointing at me, laughing."

"So, you decided to shoot him?"

"Damned right. I'd a killed that son of a bitch if they hadn't called the law."

"You do realize you are having withdrawals from alcohol and probably hallucinating."

He pointed; his hand trembled. "I ain't hallucinating. I'll admit I been drinking too much. Been making it myself for months. I won't tell them where either, but that little man, he's real!"

"Okay, did the little man say anything else to you?"

"Nah, just laughing. I'm going to blow that mother fucker to hell when I get out of here."

"I just need you to sign. The sooner you sign, and get back to the unit, the sooner they can let you out so you can take care of your business."

His signature had been shaky, too, like an elderly person with Parkinson's. It was good he would get treatment, dry out, but unless he made a different choice, I suspected he'd be back, like most of them.

"Bennett" I yelled up the stairs.

"Yes sir?"

"Does your little man laugh at you?"

"No sir, daddy. You know I am just pretending, right?"

"Get your shoes and we'll go back to the grocery, so you can get another car for your little man."

A Miracle

As we arrived in Gulf Shores, I was impressed. Despite the oil rigs visible off shore, the Southern Alabama coast seemed clean in contrast to rural Mississippi we'd traveled through from Western Tennessee. There had been a stretch of highway for hours with no sign of civilization, including gas stations or restrooms, and I feared the banjo music I might hear, thanks to Dickey, if I turned onto dirt side roads to use nature's facilities.

When we turned onto Ocean Drive, we rolled down the windows and took in the sea air. The sun had disappeared, and we craned our necks in search of our condo complex among the high rises. What we spotted were electric signs banning alcohol from the beach and flashing blue lights everywhere, vehicles pulled over into the sand and shell shoulders, teens standing behind vehicles in bathing suits while dogs sniffed to point out drugs. On rental house balconies, crowds stood, holding cups, occasionally dancing to blaring music, fraternity or sorority flags flapping in the sea breeze, and I kept thinking the balconies might collapse. Fortunately for us, our condo was at the end of the peninsula, was gated, and only reserved for families or retirees.

We were pleased with our well-decorated condo: its cleanliness, the view, and the quietness. Even the seclusion and more natural setting was relaxing and worth the extra money we'd paid. During the day, we drank plenty of water, got sun, read books, walked along the beach, or enjoyed the pool. The kids played ball with other kids on the beach, splashed or waded into the sea, or jumped in and floated and swam around the pool. We left the compound in the evening for dinner and tried to find local places that served fresh seafood for dinner and places that weren't as crowded as chain restaurants. Each evening when we ventured, it was tough to explain to the kids what was going on with the police, why dogs were sniffing cars, why teens not much older than them stood in bathing suits wearing handcuffs.

Memories of my own deviant behavior and guilt from hiding my past repeatedly swept over me, like recurring small waves. I recalled piling into a Pinto with others from my junior high, guests of our Biology teacher, an unmarried woman who always wore prescription sun glasses, even indoors, and rumored to have been a lesbian. She was the yearbook sponsor and smoked in her office along with the Math teacher whose classroom was adjacent. If we didn't have cigarettes, we could bum them from Ms. Deidra and go into the darkroom, where we developed our pictures for the yearbook, and smoked. Occasionally when we had extra money, we'd buy Ms. Deidra a pack of Vantage to repay her. When we could get someone to buy us liquor, we'd hide it in the darkroom by popping out a square tile in the ceiling. Each of us involved with the yearbook had our preferences: Seagram's 7, Bacardi rum, Relska vodka, among others. None of us smoked Vantage like Ms. Deidra. We smoked Marlboro or Camel. We had a radio in the darkroom and played music, mostly 70s music of the day, singing and dancing as the photos came out of developer, went into the finisher, and then were fastened by clothespins to a wire running the length of the room.

None of us questioned Ms. Deidra's lack of ethics or morals. We felt free, able to do what we wanted. When she offered to take some of us to the beach for the weekend, our parents all let us go. After all, she was a school teacher and advisor to those of us who were on the yearbook staff. They gave us enough money to cover our portion of the rooms, food, and some spending money, and we spent it. We began drinking when were out of the town limits, and three and a half hours later, we were cruising into Panama City Beach and checking into the Miracle Strip motel---Ms. Deidra and the girls in one room and the boys in another. After we were good and drunk, we played miniature golf just down the road, losing our clubs among the dinosaurs. We stumbled back to the Miracle Strip occasionally singing songs from *Saturday Night Fever* or *Grease* and trying to strut. We drank more until we passed out. When the sun came up, we stumbled to the beach where we drank more and passed out in the sun. By the time we came to, we were burned more than a human body should be, spending the rest of the time sick in our beds, vomiting and shaking. At some point, someone carved our names, and that we'd puked there, in the wooden headboard. Periodically, Ms. Deidra sent someone to check on us boys. By the time we left Panama City, we had sobered and somewhat recovered, but the next week we were shedding skin like snakes.

At the end of the school year, we moved on to the high school as sophomores, and for whatever reason, Ms. Deidra left the junior high and moved. None of us would have ratted on her for smoking, drinking, or even being a lesbian, if she was. We continued to party, but we moved into new circles and groups. We got jobs and when we graduated high school, we all went to college. Since we'd had such a grand time in junior high, we weren't as interested in the party scene as we got older. Unfortunately, Ms. Deidra continued to be and we later heard she had been killed in a head on collision, weaving into the other lane and killing a family with young children.

I pay close attention to the drunks in traffic on the way back to the condo after dinner. Anecdotally, I have always heard parents get paid back twice as much for their own shenanigans by their children, and I am hoping and praying this is not true. I hope by their not finding out about my behavior, they will not do anything wrong. It's probably unrealistic, but I can still hope for a miracle.

It Will Get Worse

Our first child and one-year-old daughter Rebecca wasn't feeling well and seemed to be warm. My wife Sandy took her temperature and she registered 101 in her ear. Personally, I was pleased they had invented a newer thermometer from the rectal one I'd experienced as a child. We got her into the pediatrician within an hour and they swabbed her and gave us the diagnosis—flu. I had no idea how she might have caught the flu. I wanted to blame someone - nasty germ ridden people hacking in the grocery store aisles, good Christians at church spreading Christmas cheer germs with their hugs, handshakes, and sprays of nasal mist sneezes, or worse, one of us passing it to her from someone at our places of employment. Sandy and I felt fine, so I ruled us out.

We needed to make sure Rebecca stayed hydrated, and we rotated meds between Tylenol and Motrin every four hours to help keep the fever down and let her rest. We didn't know what else to do and couldn't believe there wasn't something else in modern times that could get rid of the flu. We kept her in the baby bed, turned the humidifier on low, and kept the monitor on at night to make sure we heard any noise.

I'd had the flu a few times in my life and remember the fever, feeling weak, hallucinations of cartoon characters, mostly Wilma Flintstone and Betty Rubble. I remembered grandmothers and my parents wiping my face and forehead with a damp cloth, holding my hand, praying, eyebrows angled up with concern. Periodically, I could hear my younger siblings peaking in and asking if I would die and I heard shushes from my grandmothers and parents. I mused this was the most exciting thing that had happened in our family since the gathering to watch the moon landing, which my grandmother swore was filmed in Hollywood, another trick to turn us away from God. There were times when I had the flu that I thought I would die and I had the same dream over and over: I stood in a circle and was finally the one selected to board the UFO, its lights flashing and its engines humming, but before it took off, I awoke.

At 4:00 a.m., I got up to go to the restroom, peeked in on Rebecca, and then went to make coffee. I felt something cold on my feet, as if I stepped in a puddle of something spilled on the kitchen tile and turned on the light. It took me a minute to comprehend that water was everywhere in the kitchen. Instinctively, I checked the sink to make sure the water wasn't running, and it didn't take long to determine our pipes had burst from the freezing cold. I cut off the water. The kitchen, laundry room, part of our living room, with newly installed hardwood flooring, foyer, and part of our daughter's bedroom were flooded.

I woke Sandy, we moved what we could out of the path of flow. It was then I learned our house leaned about an inch. Later, I would have to hire an engineering firm to install a pier system to level the house before I could sell. Rebecca's temperature had come down, but as she got to moving around, it began to increase again. Before 7:00 a.m., I had talked with the insurance people at the toll free emergency number, and by 8:00 a.m., I had a clean-up crew ripping up my new hardwood, kitchen tile, carpet in my daughter's bedroom and placing large dehumidifiers and fans throughout the house. Our house would be in a state of disarray for at least a month before everything got repaired and put back together again. We called our families and let them know Rebecca had the flu and our house had been flooded. I threw the tree, decorations and all, into the yard, and officially canceled Christmas. I was angry, stomped around, and cursed about everything. "To hell with Christmas," I muttered.

After lunch, I saw the mailman drive away from the box and walked outside to get the mail - more Christmas cards from friends and relatives who would have a good Christmas, but underneath the cards was an official letter from the Internal Revenue Service. The certified public accountant I'd hired had apparently made an error on our taxes from the previous year and we owed two thousand dollars. I didn't believe it and just shook my head and laughed. This seemed to personify everything I had always heard about the IRS, but had been fortunate not to experience until that point. I decided to take Benadryl and take a nap. With my luck, I didn't need to leave the house.

Fortunately, Rebecca's fever broke Christmas day and she began to bounce back, running around the house and talking gibberish again. Having her back to normal made it a better Christmas, and while it took me a long time to overcome the issues with the flood damage and the IRS bill, I was appreciative it hadn't been worse. It could have been much worse and I imagined there were people all over the world who didn't have it as good as we did.

Penalties

Being an investigator was not as romantic as portrayed on crime dramas, and Captain Quincy Mason often clarified for his son and daughter how things were really investigated. After all, in his twenty years, there had only been about one homicide per year, which, though awful, wasn't nearly as many as some cities, and most of the crimes were some sort of domestic or drug-related incident that got out of hand. Mason had developed his own philosophy over the course of his career and believed most people just lose control and regret their actions. If they had simply walked away for a cooling off period, incidents would have been minimal.

When his cell went off, Captain Mason had a feeling this would be something odd; it was middle of the week, not the weekend when people get paid and have free time and get in trouble. It was a call to come to a garage instead of a residence or the park, which was a place to ride the merry-go-round by day and score sex or drugs at night. Fall in Bristol, Virginia was stunning - leaves in full-blown color, glimmering orange and red hues when the sunlight shown on them, and Mason felt it was ironic that the beauty signified death in nature. Typically, people stayed in more in the fall and winter, so crime rates declined, except shoplifting and robbery with the holidays. Captain Mason called Parks, the first officer on the scene who had been called by a garage worker.

"What you got?"

"You better bring the textbook for this one," said Officer Parks. "I ain't ever seen anything like it."

"You got me curious."

"I don't know if I can even explain it."

"E.T.A. in five."

"Yes sir."

Mason didn't believe it either. He actually had to walk to the side of the garage outside, gag a little, and take several quick fresh breaths, holding the cool air in his expanded lungs to soothe.

Once they pulled the male from the oversized barrel of oil, where engine blocks were usually soaked, they noted the victim's arms had been cut-off, possibly while he was still living, the coroner noted at the scene. Toenails were broken and had bled where the victim tried to push himself up from the bottom and sides of the rusted barrel that would have been too slippery without hands or arms to grip. The guy likely drowned from the oil in his lungs. Whoever did this was serious and wanted this fellow to suffer. From his wallet, they learned his name and address, and Captain Mason and Officer Parks drove to the small historic cottage in midtown.

No one answered and Captain Mason jimmied the door and called out, the only response coming from a limping dog wagging its tail. They learned the fellow worked for the local electric company and had no immediate family. Next door neighbors also said that his parents were deceased, the man had a brother who lived out of town, and he was active in his church and as a coach in little league and was a part time referee. He'd played college football at Virginia Tech, had been married once, had been divorced for at least ten years, and had no children. He'd adopted the dog from the local pound and was active in supporting a variety of charities in town, including the homeless shelter and food bank. This one would take time, Mason noted.

Mason interviewed the brother, co-workers at the electric company, church members, and by all accounts, he was a good guy with no enemies. Even in his house, Mason and other detectives found nothing to indicate any deviance. Funeral over, the case became a cold one, in a file folder held on the desk by a plastic paperweight with artwork from Mason's daughter Madeline made years before when she was in elementary school. When Mason was in the office, he couldn't get the armless, oil-soaked image out of his mind, and he knew the brutal removal of the fellow's arms was significant. He'd never heard of that.

Weeks later on a winter morning when a light snow had blanketed Bristol, causing schools to close, Mason came in, had a latte and banana nut muffin and decided to do some specific Google searches using quotations to see if there was a pattern emerging elsewhere. Searching for "armless" and "armless murders" didn't turn up anything that seemed to relate, except folks who were armless and had committed crimes, which he thought was odd. Plus, those crimes had been in distant places like New York or California, not in Southern Virginia and East Tennessee, so Mason continued to search. An hour later, Mason noticed an odd crime headline: "Man's Legs Sawed off and Tossed over fence at Alligator Farm in Florida."

"Good night," Mason said. "How sick."

He walked outside, propped against the stone wall, breathed in the crisp air, spoke with a few rookies coming and going, working wrecks, and he decided he'd call the St. Augustine, Florida police department just to see if he could find out anything. Mason's motto had always been to leave no stone overturned.

"Lt. Banks."

"Good morning, Lt. This is Capt. Mason with Bristol P.D. in Virginia. How're you doing?"

"Excellent, sir. Yourself?"

"Enjoying this first snow."

"You can keep that stuff up there. Plenty of sunshine here. Probably even have a drowning at the beach."

"Doesn't sound good."

"Well, it's to be expected here. Alcohol and beaches don't mix."

"Understood."

"Well, you didn't call to talk about possible drownings, so what can I do for you?"

"I want to ask you some questions about this strange case you had there. The alligator farm case."

"Oh yeah. That was gruesome. Gators will eat just about anything. It's a miracle we got much of him at all, but from what we could tell, they'd been fed earlier, so they weren't that interested in much of him. Plus, he wasn't completely fresh."

"That's interesting. We've had a strange case here, and I know it's a longshot, but I thought I'd check with you. I'm sure it's a waste of time."

"What's your case like?"

"Single male, seemingly normal life, arms cut off and left in a rusted barrel mostly filled with oil behind a garage. No connection to the garage or employees."

"Say his arms were cut off?"

"Yeah."

"What did they use?"

"Well autopsy's not definitive, so we don't know, but I would expect a chain-saw."

"If it turns out it's a chain-saw, we might have a connection."

"What about your victim?"

"Middle-aged family guy. College graduate. Church goer. Worked as a department store manager at the mall."

"No connection that I detect."

"Well, let me know what you find out. We could use a little lead ourselves."

When they hung up, Mason ran some errands in town and ran by the morgue to talk with the coroner to see if he had any new evidence. The visit turned out to be more social than work-related, though the coroner, too, suspected a chain saw based on the cut. He also noted it was likely he was cut somewhere else and taken to the garage due to the amount of blood splatter on his clothes and the dirt and leaf debris embedded in his jeans, likely from being dragged. Mason didn't want to think about a serial killer on the loose with a chain saw. It dredged memories of the movie from the 1970s, a movie he hadn't liked.

That evening, Mason's family watched a rerun of a University of Tennessee football game, and they were excited about attending the upcoming game between the U.T. Volunteers and the University of Georgia Bulldogs. Neither team had performed well in recent years, and often the coach was the recipient of blame. This year, though, both teams were doing well, and predictions were all over the map. Mason was excited they'd scored tickets and would travel two hours to Knoxville to see the game.

Their children did their homework in their rooms after dinner. Mason knew they were good kids. He and Sandy had been blessed in that regard. Mason had been a bit deviant when he was growing up in Bristol, an old mountain town known for its musical origins from the Carter family and also known for racing. Sandy, on the other hand, had grown up in a large farming family at the base of the mountains in East Tennessee where land was fertile from run-off and made for a productive farm. Sandy had gone to a private Presbyterian college in Bristol while Mason had gone through the police academy and ultimately received an Associate's degree in Criminal Justice from a community college, but to get promoted, he had to finish his Bachelor's in the evening at the university in Johnson City, a short drive from Bristol. He was appreciative that the police department had reimbursed tuition and books for the program and hearing from friends how much debt some of them had incurred, he was also appreciative that Sandy had received a scholarship and what that didn't cover, her parents had paid. The only debt they had was their house and they felt it might be paid off in just a few more years. Madeline and Austin were both good kids, and Mason was able to keep tabs on their friends to make sure they weren't running with the wrong crowd or moving into any deviant circles.

Mason retired early and awoke about three in the morning to a dreadful dream about the armless man in the oil barrel. He dreamed he was that man, he could hear the chainsaw, and then could feel the oil coating his lungs, and he woke up sweating and almost thought he heard a chainsaw off in the woods behind their house. He got up, trying not to wake Sandy, went to the kitchen, and drank a glass of ice water. He sat in the recliner in the den, covered up with a throw, and dozed. Sandy woke him when she got up earlier than the alarm and wondered where he was.

"You couldn't sleep?"

"No, I slept, but woke up from a dream about this case."

"You can't always solve everything. You know that."

"I know, but I'll solve this one. It may take a few years though"

"Want some coffee?"

"Yes, strong. I'll need it today."

Mason headed to work earlier than usual, rounded a curve, and almost hit a doe in the middle of the road. Fortunately, the early November snow had melted off before sundown or he likely would have slid the unmarked cruiser right into the doe, killing her and doing major damage to the vehicle's front end.

Once in his office, he called Lt. Banks in St. Augustine.

"Banks."

"Good morning. This is Mason in Bristol calling again."

"Good to hear from you. How are the leaves up there? Sure would like to see them. May have to wait until I retire."

"You're welcome to come here anytime. Be glad to show you around. The full color was in October, and it's something I always enjoy."

"Well, you didn't call to talk about the leaves, I know."

"Coroner says it looks like it might have been a chainsaw."

"Hmm. Now we need to figure out what these two guys have in common."

"I'll scan and email you the file to look at. I'll be down in Knoxville tomorrow for the Tennessee-Georgia game."

"Oh, that will be a good one. I'll be watching it on TV. Hopefully, there will be some others worth watching. I won't bother you over the weekend, but I'll give you a call if I see something. Tell you what. I'll have Felicia scan and email you our guy's file, so you can look at it and see if you see anything that might connect."

"Sounds good. I appreciate it."

"Sure thing. See ya."

The file arrived in Mason's inbox late in the afternoon when he was getting ready to shut down his computer and head home for an early dinner before the early morning drive to Knoxville, and he didn't look at it.

Before sunrise, family members stumbled around the kitchen and snapped at each other. None of them had slept enough because of late night movies, so everyone had coffee and loaded into the vehicle with velour throws. Once Mason was on interstate 81 headed toward Knoxville, the rest of the family napped while he sipped coffee and watched the sun rise over the mountains. The blanket of frost created a mist as the sun warmed the fields.

As they got closer to Knoxville and as Mason began to slow because of heavy traffic, they heard the rumbling and gearing down of trucks and everyone stirred. At least two hours before kick-off, Mason parked and the four visited a group of officers and their families who were tailgating. They snacked, and Mason enjoyed conversation about the game while Sandy talked with other wives about retirement and travel. Madeline and Austin sat in orange lawn chairs, heads bowed toward phones. When kick-off was a bit closer, the crowd put away food, loaded coolers in truck beds, and folded chairs and placed them in the truck cabs. The crowd shuffled up the ramps, and Mason turned back and looked out at the Tennessee River and the view of the rolling hills and downtown, and it was a stunning view. Sandy complained her legs were hurting and the kids laughed and told her she should exercise more. When they finally found their seats, the stadium had nearly filled, and Mason noted that this was not the ideal place to watch a game from a security standpoint and was the perfect place for a terrorist attack. He also thought it was a shame he had such an idea. Twenty years prior such would have never crossed his mind.

A few hours of roaring crowds with scores from both teams, several crowd waves, and some more rabid fans standing up and hollering at referees, the game came to an end with a score of

Tennessee 42 and Georgia 21. The Georgia coach was clearly disappointed, hanging his head and sprinting off the field with a sea of red. The big orange coach, on the other hand, told reporters they had talked about what they would need to do to pull off a win and he was pleased they had done it.

Clearly, it had been the best game of the season for UT and Mason was glad they'd come.

The game had been Georgia's worst loss of the season. A run from a punt of 80 yards, a touchdown from kick-off, and multiple off-sides, clipping, and face mask penalties had cost Georgia several points in the game. At some point during the game, Mason became aware he was not focused on the game so much as he was running mental scenarios about his victim and wished he'd read the file sent to him from Florida before leaving work.

It had taken them two hours to get out of the stadium, the parking lot, and get back into steady traffic on the interstate headed back toward Bristol. Mason decided that he would drop the family off at their house, grab a quick bite to eat, and head over to the office to check the file. Once in his office, he ran through the file, and there didn't seem to be anything that jumped out at him, though the victim clearly had his legs removed in advance of being tossed into the pit at the alligator farm. It seemed to Mason this could be a mafia-like crime, something that he'd read happened a lot in New York and New Jersey, and with the influx of Northerners into Florida, he assumed there had been mafia who relocated there as well. He sent an email back to Lt. Banks that he didn't see any connection and Banks had replied to Mason's email that he'd looked over Mason's file and didn't see a connection either. So, Mason felt he'd reached a dead-end.

A few months later while Mason sat in his boxers and t-shirt watching headline news, the strangest crime story he'd ever heard was reported. Apparently, a body was uncovered in Tuscaloosa, Alabama along the river bank. The victim's face had been removed, but there were no other injuries. Police were still working the case and had no comment, which Mason thought appropriate, but several community members had comments including one robust fellow who maintained if the "Face Eater" came around his house, he'd be ready with the shotgun. Mason shook his head, but given the type of crime, he knew the labeling of the perpetrator as a "Face Eater" was what would get picked up and run over and over in the media.

A couple of days later, Mason caught a glimpse of the news in the lobby at the station as he walked in, and he stopped, motioned to the desk sergeant to turn up the volume, and they offered an update of the fellow who they'd found by the river. He had once worked for the University of Alabama in the football program, and the report relayed the coach and football team would be pall bearers in his funeral. The victim had stayed in Tuscaloosa through the years after having been a successful running back under Bear Bryant, had helped financially support players from his earnings as a pub owner, had served as a fill-in referee locally, and had attended all home games and practices.

Mason wondered if the fellow had been robbed after the closing of the pub late at night and somehow was cut or maimed and then thrown onto the river bank where maybe a bobcat or some other animal might have come along having been attracted to the blood and ate his face. Regardless, Mason made the call to Tuscaloosa and got Lt. Garrett.

"Lt. Garrett here."

"Lt. Garrett, this is Capt. Mason at Bristol P.D. in Virginia. How're you doing?"

"Good sir, you?"

"Fine, thanks. Sorry to bother you, but I wondered if you would mind sharing anything about your recent case of the faceless fellow."

"Yes, sir, well, before we have that conversation, I'm looking you up on the website to see if you're legit."

"Well, it's nice to see someone checking on this. I tell my guys all the time that they'll get calls from family, reporters, what have you, and they should always verify and check it out."

"Sorry, Captain. Looks like you're legit. We've been getting tons of calls trying to get information. Now, how can I help you?"

"I was curious if there was a connection between your case of the faceless victim and a murder we had here in Bristol."

"Well, I can tell you this much. We've never seen anything like it. At first, we thought he might have been shot or stabbed after closing his pub and dumped and an animal did that, but there were no cuts or gunshot wounds anywhere else on his body. Then we thought he might have had a heart attack, but coroner says he bled out from his juggler, which was sliced in the removal of his face. He was carved up like a Christmas turkey. We haven't ever seen anything like this."

"Whoever did this was a serious psycho."

"You got it."

"Any other clues or pieces of evidence?"

"There was a yellow penalty flag found in the mud near the victim, but we don't think it has anything to do with it."

"Well, I appreciate it, Lt. Garrett. Our victim was found in an oil barrel with his arms cut off. The poor fellow drowned in the oil. We have nothing. I'm just checking on anything that is bizarre. Maybe one of these days, I'll figure it out."

"Good luck to you, sir."

"Thanks. You, too."

Mason went to lunch in the downtown diner, the meat and three as locals referred to it, with the Uncle Billy's lunch club, which was a group the Chief had invited him to join. In fact, the only way anyone could sit at the table with the others in the club was to be invited. The group consisted of a variety of leaders in the community: the mayor, a city council member, the fire and police chief, a business owner, a college president, the newspaper editor, and a judge. The group didn't talk a lot about the daily issues that arose in their respective areas of employment so much as they tried to solve world problems and talk about politics. Mason didn't say much and the Chief knew he was in deep thought.

"Everything alright?" the chief asked.

"Yep, just thinking about that murder," Mason responded.

"It'll come. Just takes time."

"I know. I just don't like waiting."

They both chuckled and Mason took off to the garage. He thought he might poke around again. He hadn't been in a while, and they had combed the area more than once searching for any clues.

Once parked, Mason let the young lady in the office know he was there and waved at the mechanics. He leaned by a tree near the oil barrel and sent a couple of text replies to emails, one of which was to his daughter who had sent him a picture of a convertible she wanted. He'd replied that they would discuss it later. The sun was glistening on the new fallen snow out behind the garage, and Mason noted the light reflecting on trash sporadically located around the crime scene. As he focused on each piece, he saw what he thought was a yellow leaf sticking out of the snow in the stand of trees. As he made his way around car parts and the oil barrel, Mason slipped on a plastic glove he kept in his pocket, pulled, and realized the yellow was what looked like a penalty flag. He put the flag in a plastic bag he pulled from his pocket, checked the immediate area, and walked back to his unmarked cruiser and headed straight for the lab. Mason didn't want to get his hopes up, but he felt this might be the break he needed. He also called Lt. Banks in St. Augustine on his way back to the station, shared about the victim in Tuscaloosa and the flag, and shared he'd gone back to the scene and found what appeared to be a penalty flag. Lt. Banks vowed he would go to the alligator farm and see if there was any sort of evidence again. Mason suggested they share their files with Tuscaloosa P.D. and have a conference call, asserting if they put their minds together, they could get closer to discovery. Mason called Garrett in Tuscaloosa and he agreed to the conference call the next afternoon.

Mason let his chief know immediately after getting back into his office.

"What do you think?"

"I don't know yet."

"What do the crimes have in common?"

"The victims are all white males and single."

"Think it's a homosexual crime?"

"No, nothing indicates that."

"Anything else?"

"You know, our victim played football for Virginia Tech. The Tuscaloosa victim played for Alabama."

"What about the St. Augustine victim?"

"It wasn't in the file."

"2 penalty flags?"

"Yes."

"What about the crimes?"

"Well, our victim was missing his arms. The one in Alabama had his face cut off, and the one in Florida had his legs cut off."

"What's the penalty?"

"Sir?"

"Do those relate to penalties?"

"Not that I can see."

"What happened to our victim?"

"Sir, they cut off his arms."

"Off sides?"

"Good night! That's it. The one in Alabama would be face masking and the one in Florida - clipping? Thanks, chief."

Mason grinned, shook his head, and laughed as he headed across the hall to his office. Barely sitting in his desk chair, Mason's cell rang and he noted it was Lt. Banks.

"Got a penalty flag," Banks said. "It was buried under a little mud, only a portion sticking out. Just didn't appear a clue to anyone at the scene, I guess. There's something else."

"What?"

"Our victim played for Miami. I don't believe it's in the file. Didn't seem relevant at the time."

"Excellent," Mason said. "Now, we've got to connect the dots. What a break-through day. I didn't think we'd get here."

"Me neither."

"So," Mason said. "Since he's leaving penalty flags, I am assuming we are either looking for a psychotic football player who played against each of these teams and had an issue with these players or a referee. We have some homework to do."

"It's going to be tough. We probably need to pull in the FBI, too, given the crimes cross multiple state lines. The FBI can help with their resources."

"Right. I don't know how we'll go through all this game footage, but clearly this killer is about the penalties. I guess in his world he was wronged by these former players. I don't know how a referee would be involved."

"Me neither. Alright then. We'll talk tomorrow. Thanks."

"Sure. Have a great evening."

"It will be at some level, but we *have* a serial killer out there."

Sandy was glad to hear there had been a breakthrough, glad to see Mason's worried look disappear. Mason slept like a baby, felt exceptional when he woke, had coffee, and left early. When he got to the office, he made calls to the regional FBI office in Richmond and left a message for them to call giving them some detail, so they could coordinate with Florida and Alabama agents. He also made a call to the TBI in Nashville for their assistance.

By mid-morning, two FBI agents - Tom Harris and Dale Rettig - set up operations at Bristol P.D. and Mason shared his and Lt. Banks' files.

He also invited them to sit in on his conference call with Banks and Garrett that afternoon. Both agents were very complimentary of their work, especially picking up on the flag clues as well as the identifying the football penalties connected to the particular crimes.

Later, Mason, Banks, and Garrett had the conference call and the FBI agents sat in and suggested Banks and Garrett come to Bristol, where they could be of more value to the team. Both agreed and made arrangements to be in Bristol the next day. Harris and Rettig had folks in Richmond pull football footage for the three teams during the years the victims played. Interestingly, all three had been decent football players and held good records. It was tedious going through the records, and they found no penalties among them during the first year of video footage they were able to secure and watch, but then, this had been their freshman years and they had not had as much playing time at that point in their careers. It was not until the junior year that they found the first penalty by the Virginia Tech. player. His reaction to the player he faced as well as to the referee was rather volatile, behavior that Mason felt was not in character with all the information they had collected in his file. Nonetheless, he understood how in younger years, males tend to be more high strung and aggressive than once they settle down in life. The player had reacted in such a negative fashion that they had ejected him from the game, and other players had to hold him back and guide him off the field. The crowd of Virginia Tech fans had booed at the call, but after the next play was set in motion, the fans had calmed.

Agents Harris and Rettig and Mason continued on into the early evening and just before 8:00 p.m., they found what they thought might be the clipping penalty the Miami player made against the Florida Gator player. This player, too, was volatile and knocked down the Gator until the referee and others from the Hurricane team pulled him away at which point he began to poke the referee in the chest and scream obscenities. Agents marked and printed off both the Gator player's photo with identifying jersey number and also printed off the referee's picture. Through the victim's senior year, there were minor infractions on the team, but nothing nearly as volatile. The same was the case with the Virginia Tech player. It seemed either they learned valuable lessons from their behavior or they simply listened to their coaches for fear of retribution. The men gave up at 10:00 PM and decided to wait and go through the Alabama footage the next morning when they felt more fresh.

Mason felt like they would get a breakthrough by the next morning. On the way home, he found it interesting that, if the culprit was a player, they were looking at more than one, which he thought unlikely. The penalty against the Virginia Tech victim had been made when playing Georgia and the penalty against the Miami victim had been made while playing the Florida Gators. He also thought it was interesting that the Miami player had been fed to gators, literally. Mason was dog-tired and slept well. The next morning, he left early and drank strong coffee before the agents came to the office.

They viewed the footage up until, again, a volatile play with the Alabama victim face-masking a player from the Tennessee Vols, a game that had gone down in history between coaches Bear Bryant and Johnny Majors. The Big Orange had stopped the Crimson Tide by only a few points and while the face mask penalty hadn't made a major difference, it was a spectacle to watch with the Volunteer starting a fight with the victim. A referee had been punched in the face by the Alabama victim and was removed by medical personnel for a check before he came back in the game. The FBI agents looked at each other and Mason and said in unison, "The referee." Mason's hunch had been right: three penalties to different players did not equal one serial killer. If the referee was the same in all three games, they needed to move fast, since they had no idea who would be next.

The agents and Mason decided to eat lunch at the diner, but didn't sit with the club members. After a quick lunch, they met Banks and Garrett in the lobby. They made the introductions and then moved back to the work room where agents and Mason caught them up to speed. Banks and Garrett were impressed, especially after watching the specific footage.

"That was quick work, guys," Banks said.

"Well, when you have all this snow, you don't have anything else to do, but work, unlike watching bikinis at the beach," Mason joked and they all laughed.

The problem with referees was that they were typically anonymous to players and coaches in an attempt to avoid harassment from players or fans and were often escorted to and from games. The standard uniforms, too, helped remove some of the more personal characteristics one might detect. While the group waited for information from Richmond to help identify the referee, they put together a profile with multiple characteristics they knew the killer would have based on other profiles and they discussed how they might approach. Depending on location, Mason, Garrett, and Banks might not be authorized for action; however, they were welcome to accompany the FBI agents.

Harris and Rettig asked if Mason could get them a plane locally in Bristol to avoid the process of getting one sent from headquarters in Richmond. One of the few private jets docked at Bristol's airport was owned by the Kodak family and used primarily by the family and the photography company in the Tri-cities area. With a promise of reimbursement from federal or local agencies, Mason secured the Learjet, which held eight and was ready at any given notice.

Even with media hounding Tuscaloosa police, Garrett had not shared he was in Bristol working with others on the case, and it hadn't leaked from St. Augustine or Bristol or from Richmond, yet, but they knew it was a matter of time before something leaked and media swarmed.

At 3:00 P.M. and after multiple gyrations of research angles, Richmond agents called to say the suspect in at least two seemed a match to a retired Department of Natural Resources officer named Emory Serbenski. From what intelligence had gathered, Serbenski had played college football at Clemson and completed a degree in Natural Resources, had been picked up by the pro circuit, the AFL, had played before an injury took him out. He'd returned to the Newberry, South Carolina area and worked in the Sumter National Forest. Mason called the airport to let them know they needed to get as close to Newberry as possible while FBI agents called field offices in Greenville to meet them at the Newberry airport. The airport wasn't used at all for commercial traffic and mostly housed small, private aircraft. The pilot and co-pilot were concerned about runway length, but also knew this was high priority. They felt it would work if they adjusted landing and take-off speeds. The weather was clear in most of the state of South Carolina, so they felt comfortable with their decision.

Once in the air, officers were quiet and occasionally discussed details. Mason learned from the FBI data that Serbenski had been married, but his wife had succumbed to cancer after a long battle. They could find no religious or social organization connections for Serbenski, and the couple had one adopted daughter from South America who was married and had a successful career on the West Coast. While he had been a substitute referee for a number of years with the

Southeastern Conference (SEC), he had retired from the DNR once his wife had become sick. Mason hoped they had the right guy. He certainly fit the typical profile: white male, loner, and no close family.

When the plane landed, there were several unmarked cars waiting and they were driven to the destination. It was determined Mason would accompany the FBI to the Serbenski house, a brick ranch on several acres that adjoined the forest. They had secured a warrant, and as they approached, the other vehicles hung back just off the road on the shoulder. The house was dark and there wasn't a car in the double carport on the back, but as they approached the front door, outside security lights came on, a barking dog came running around the house, the front porch light came on, and the wooden door creaked open a little.

"FBI. Open the door."

A gentleman was squinting at the light shown in his eyes. "What'd you say?"

"FBI. Open up!"

The door completely opened and the agents told him to turn around and put his hands on the wall. It was clear he didn't have a weapon because he was wearing boxers and a t-shirt. "Mr. Serbenski, you are under arrest."

"I'm not Serbenski," the man said. "Name's Earl Howard. Wallet's on the kitchen table." Mason walked over, peaked in, and confirmed.

"Where's Serbenski?"

"I don't know. Said he was moving to the coast around Hilton Head."

"Did he used to be here?"

"Yeah, I bought the house last year. Don't even know him, but I took the job here with DNR and this was a perfect location for me."

After checking around, and after the South Carolina officers verified, the group was back at the airport, trying to get any leads as to where Serbenski might have gone. Richmond researchers were in communication with agents as the jet took off again for the short flight to Hilton Head. While they learned Serbenski had no forwarding address, they did learn his pension checks were being sent to a post office box on Dawtaw Island, a small island closer to Beaufort than Hilton Head, and they directed the pilots to make the adjustment. They also radioed ahead for cars. What they learned upon landing is that no one knew Serbenski, but they knew he came to the Post Office and grocery store periodically. They further learned from Richmond that paychecks were being deposited in a bank account from a research corporation that owned a small island referred to by locals as Monkey Island. Calls to the company confirmed he was the only employee on the island and his job consisted of feeding, testing the monkeys, collecting data, and reporting back. They were cautioned that the monkeys carried diseases and a scratch could contaminate.

Local officers pointed out where the dock and boat were, and if Serbenski were on the island in the lab, connected to a small cabin, it would be easy for him to swim to Dawtaw to escape. Local officers also shared they could all fit in one boat and would position themselves on different parts of the island with silencers and darts in case the monkeys tried to attack. This would also work to take out Serbenski. While they still had a couple of hours of daylight, Mason was nonetheless concerned, mostly for the safety of the others. None of them, aside from the locals, had ever been on a mission in a South Carolina marsh, and none of them had experience with monkeys.

After each man was deposited, the local officers felt they should go ashore away from the dock, so to keep the boat out of site. Harris, Rettig, and Mason, climbed out, holding a branch of a Live Oak tree covered in moss, and bent down. They could see the cabin and what appeared to be movement inside. Taking positions behind the Live Oak trees, it didn't take long to spot Serbenski walking by a window with a bottle of water. Screams of monkeys from the other side of the island seemed to alert Serbenski. He put on his shirt, grabbed a gun, and walked to the front door, sprinting onto the porch and walking to the other side, where the monkey screams originated, his back facing the FBI agents and Mason. Mason aimed the gun directly for Serbenski's leg, and the dart landed square in the back of his leg, the force of which knocked him off the porch into the sand below. As he moaned from the sedative swimming swiftly through his system, the agents were on him, cuffing him and reading him rights before he could get up and grab his gun.

Once Harris and Rettig had him cuffed and on his feet, his eyes met Mason's.

"Good call. Interference," Serbenski said.

"How many?" Mason asked.

"Four," Serbenski said.

"Why'd you do it?"

"I don't know."

As Serbenski became groggier, Harris and Rettig loaded him on the boat to circle and pick up the others and head back to shore. Mason wondered if Serbenski would offer up the fourth penalty victim.

Reading the Coffee Grounds

My eccentric aunt, now in her mid-eighties and who finally quit smoking last year after a bout with pneumonia and colon cancer, sits and watches TV around the clock in her bedroom at her daughter's house, fanning herself with a funeral home fan adorned with the owner's photo. McLane is a lean, dark-haired fellow sporting a two-piece poplin khaki suit, two-toned bucks, and a madras tie. "We care for the whole family" is the slogan on the fan, and while most of us cynics recognize the not-so-subtle marketing concept, my aunt has long passed the slogan and has established a relationship with McLane. She has lengthy conversations with him, telling him about her life, apparently hearing about his. When winter finally arrived, my cousin took the fan one day when my aunt dozed, and she cried and thought he'd left her, as her two husbands had done. My cousin, who my aunt believes is a friend from childhood, brought the fan back to her and my aunt scolded her and held McLane close. The dementia has pushed my aunt one step closer to visiting McLane's business.

Knowing my aunt - and the rest of us - will one day pass doesn't make accepting death any easier. When I learned my aunt's friend and one time neighbor Jackie had passed, from FaceBook of all places, I had smiled, not because she had passed, but because of the reading of coffee grounds by her twenty years ago, which left a lasting impression.

Jackie was a twin to Jill and both women were plump, had beautiful soprano voices, short-cropped gray hair, and what fascinated me most was that they were missing several of the same teeth. They seem to always wear what my mother called homemade tent dresses and sandals - tennis shoes or boots in the winter.

Jackie and Jill lived on the property to the West of my aunt's, set back further off the town street and nestled behind a stand of cedars. From the road, passersby could not view the unfinished ranch house wrapped in tar paper, or the engines, old cars, a boat, appliances, and other non-functioning things dispersed about the property. Jackie and Jill's father, I was told, was an engineer who had once worked at NASA, but as I looked about the place, I couldn't imagine it true. Jackie and Jill both had several children, with no visible fathers, and seemed simple and captivated by us. My siblings and I only came to visit for a day or two out of the year. Likewise, we were fascinated by them, by the way they lived, and by the way they acted happy despite their poverty. My siblings and I were afraid of them, as if associating with them would pull us into their world and keep us prisoners. We imagined them lurking outside my aunt's house at night, trying to get in and steal us away. That, combined with my aunt's unpainted clapboard siding in the dark, made for some imaginary evil.

When I was in college, I was passing by the small town just off the interstate where my aunt lived and decided to stop. I forewarned my friend who was with me that my aunt was a bit strange. Her car was parked in the shade of the Live Oaks in the circular dirt driveway. She was sitting on the screened side porch drinking coffee and smoking. "Hey, hey," she yelled. "I'll be damned. I thought I'd never see you again." That was her guilt trip and I laughed and shifted the conversation, introducing my friend Grant. We visited awhile, and she talked about the power of crystals, spirit guides, and herbal healing when we heard some rustling in the hedges and then a "Yoo-hoo, anybody home?"

"Jackie, come look see what dragged up," my aunt yelled. "You recall my nephew Kevin, and he's brought his smart college friend Grant with him."

Jackie giggled, "I sure do. How you doing Kevin? Good to meet you Grant." Jackie had on a tent dress, sandals, and held a Bible in her hand with all sorts of papers stuck in it.

"Victoria," Jackie said to my aunt. "I've found some verses I wanted to share." Part of me wondered if Jackie was witnessing to my aunt, but my aunt's rolling her eyes indicated to me she tolerated the visit because she had nothing else to do and certainly tolerated her more than the Jehovah Witnesses who she had threatened with her machete if they didn't get off her property.

"Get in the porch before the bugs tote you off. Why don't you get some coffee and give Kevin and his friend a reading." She turned to me and Grant. "I'll get you a cup and you sip it. That will help Jackie sense you in the grounds."

I looked at Grant who had a perplexed look on his face, and I could tell I would hear about this later. Aunt Victoria returned with cups, both fine ceramic-ware giveaways from local businesses. We sipped coffee while Victoria and Jackie gossiped about other neighbors and community members. When we finished, we were directed to place our mugs upside-down, so the grounds would dry and create a pattern. Apparently, the pattern would give Jackie psychic information as well.

Jackie picked up my cup and stared into it, smiled, and said, "Oh, this is interesting. I see eagles flying high above a mountain city; you're speaking to a crowd of people below. I see you are surrounded by the wise ones, guiding you." She stopped and put the cup down. "I think you are an old soul," she said, "and you've done this all before."

I didn't know what I thought of reincarnation then, but it seemed unlikely to me. She did a different reading for Grant, seeing motifs and totem animals and talking more about adventures. When Grant and I said our goodbyes, I knew it would be a while before we visited my aunt and her friend Jackie again. In fact as the years passed, I only saw my aunt a handful of times at funerals or reunions and didn't see Jackie again. All these years later, I wonder about the readings and the reality. Truth is, I went on to graduate school and worked in colleges and gave talks to large groups and Grant traveled the world, becoming a pilot, and had a great deal of adventures, including safaris.

Coincidence, planting seeds that germinated and grew, or reality, I didn't know, but the reading was interesting and fun. I still wonder if someone had the ability to see the future why she wouldn't change her own.

Birthday Present

for Margaret

The base had slowed for the holiday season; many of the officers and enlisted had driven, or taken the shuttle to Atlanta to fly, home. A core remained to keep the base operational and to be on stand-by in case Gorbachchev pushed the button in Moscow or if Reagan decided we would strike first. An undercurrent of suspicion between nations was in the air, and while we watched the F4's rumble into the Southern sky, fire shooting from their engines, we felt safe and gathered in the World War II Billeting barracks for an exchange of gifts under five dollars and to celebrate with multicultural hors-d'oeuvres: boiled peanuts, pecan bars, Swiss cookies, chips and salsa, minced fish in pastries, fruit with raisins and egg rolls. Someone made Santa punch, a red concoction with vodka.

Most of the group brought their spouses and had a drink or two, but Jerry, who worked in the Services squadron, brought a blind friend named Chuck, and they downed multiple cups of punch. Jerry's wife Imelda, who was from the Philippines and worked there as a maid, took a break to join the festivities. Blind Chuck told the crowd he could see shadows and sometimes detect a difference in textures. At some point, we learned it was Chuck's birthday, and we all sang and he tried to hug and thank us, his alcohol induced hysteria turned to weeps and sobs, like so many drunks. As Jerry led him out, others were gathering up their dollar store gifts and helping pick up paper plates and cups, combing crumbs off furniture, and sweeping, I thought I saw blind Chuck get behind the wheel and quickly commented to others who laughed and dismissed my perception as alcohol related.

As I drove past the security police station and off base, I notice the flashing lights and slowed to see Jerry and Chuck were cuffed and standing next to the police car while the mangled Thunderbird rested cattywampass in the ditch. I'm sure as the other party goers passed, they were thankful they'd had only one or two drinks.

The early paper didn't run the story, so I thought they probably arrested Jerry for DUI and I had been wrong about blind Chuck driving, but the evening news picked up the story and it even made its way to CNN Headline News: Blind Man Arrested for DUI. Wolf Blitzer struggled to keep giggles at bay when he recounted that Jerry wanted to give Chuck a birthday gift and learned Chuck had always wanted to drive even though he clearly couldn't. Jerry thought he could manage the one mile trek to the Spanish Mission apartment complex with Jerry as guide, but they were so drunk and got tickled when Chuck didn't slow at the base gate and broke the wooden arm, tires screeching onto the highway.

The next week, Imelda was cleaning at the Billeting office and said, "Crazy GI. I told him blind man trouble. Now trouble come to my house." Ellen, the manager of Billeting, shared if it was discovered we had the alcohol at the party, we'd all be in the doghouse with the base commander. As Imelda swept, Reagan delivered a Christmas message on TV, warning the Soviets and hoping for peace on Earth.

Checking In

At the Ramada, Sunday from 3:00 p.m. to 11:00 p.m. was the best shift to work the desk. The travelers along the interstate were destined for their homes on Sunday. It was often slow, and the only guests who had reservations on Sundays were mostly business regulars, except Mr. Frazier, an elderly man.

"You doing okay?"

"Sure am." He was dressed in a three piece, hat, and freshly shined shoes. Reeked of Brut. "Need a single."

"Yes, sir." He always wanted a single. On the back side, so folks passing in cars didn't recognize his.

"On the back side. And here's my discount card," he said. I didn't need his card. I knew he had one. We'd gone through this routine about twice a month for the past three years.

"Yes, sir. That'll be $34.95." He already held a twenty, ten, and five, and I gave him a nickel back and handed him the key.

"Enjoy your stay," I said. Technically, he wouldn't stay. I really didn't know what to say to him. I wanted to know what he did for a living, if he went to church before coming here, if he was married or widowed, if he picked up women after church to bring to the motel for sex, beginning the new week with sin. I was curious, even fascinated, with the mysterious and deviant behavior, and it was the first time I thought of elderly and sex going together. I didn't want to imagine it or ask my grandparents. I just naturally assumed they were like the Cleavers, sleeping single in single beds.

He nodded, grinned, and went out the glass door. I watched the near perfect 1970s Chrysler pull away, disappearing behind the two-story orange brick flat roof hotel that in just a few years would be torn down and replaced with a high rise, updated to attract a newer generation of travelers, business folks, and shack jobs with continental breakfasts, mints on pillows, and coffee or hot tea in the room.

A couple of hours later, the Chrysler drove slowly by, and I sent the night maid around to clean the room. "Don't ever look messed up at all," she said. "Just an empty bottle of Mogen David and an empty Kentucky Fried Chicken bucket."

"You think they get it on, Delores?"

"Uh-huh. I think they just make the bed, so we think they don't."

"Even at their age?"

"You're crazy. You keep on till you can't and then they got medication to help."

Bus 53

After my road rage swelled and I passed the slow moving Chevy truck, I noticed the flashing yellow lights a quarter of a mile ahead on Hollywood, where dreams aren't born, but end in the city cemetery. I slowed and probably caused the Chevy driver to laugh at my impatience. Made me think of karma.

I stopped behind a long line of vehicles and watched kids of all shapes and sizes slug their way aboard the bus. They didn't rush or seem to care about the line of cars, folks rushing to get to their jobs.

It had been thirty years since I'd ridden a school bus, and I felt sure Mr. Williams, a crotchety and humped mass of a man with thin lips, horn-rimmed glasses, and a faded green tattoo on his forearm, was long dead. The only time he spoke was when kids were out of line---mostly, the football and basketball players, the river rats (a group of poor kids mean as snakes who should have been sent off to prison in elementary school since it seemed to be in their DNA), and the ranch boys (mostly mean boys given up or abandoned by their families or sent to the ranch by the courts). When his voice boomed, "Cut it out", there was silence and conformity. He didn't have to say any more. I don't think I ever heard of anyone cross or challenge him. I imagined he'd body slammed a defensive tackle from the quad-A football team in the past, and the information had been passed down from one class to the next.

Once both feet were planted on the first step, Mr. Williams slammed the folding door and stomped the gas pedal to the floor, the bus lunging forward rollicking along, the newest border stumbling down the aisle grabbing metal poles to maintain balance and find a seat. In the winter, some would let down their windows to play "Freeze Out," not so much a game since there were no winners, only losers. Usually, the bus came around sun-up, so most of us were so sleepy, we didn't pay attention to the other stops or our peers' homes. We were all poor. Anyone middle class or higher either went to a private school or their mothers shuttled them in new cars that was content for our dreams.

I mostly kept to myself and stared out the window at pine thickets, day dreaming of a different life, of what I might do when I finally got a car and didn't have to ride the bus, of imagining the heavy chested high school girl across the aisle naked, her breasts bobbing up and down like buoys in a bay. I turned my thoughts to old Ms. Stein from Geometry and Algebra. A quick vision of her was enough for any teenage boy to kill a bulge in his Levi's. Closing my eyes, I dozed, and only when Mr. Williams slammed on the brakes to turn into the school's long driveway did I wake up to people all over the bus pointing and laughing at me. Even the ranch boys and river rats were pointing and laughing. I first glanced to my crotch to make sure nothing had escaped or was standing at attention, and when the girl in front of me handed me her compact mirror, I finally got it.

My eye-lashes were longer than usual and my slightly arched eyebrows had become more triangular. Lipstick was more of an "O" above my lips and below on the chin making me a twin for Mr. Bill from *Saturday Night Live.* Even my high cheekbones were highlighted with rouge. I looked like a clown or a kid in drag, and when the bus jolted to a stop in the parking lot with all the other yellow ones, I made a dash to the bathroom to wash my face, knowing I would get a demerit for tardiness.

While no one ever confessed, and they all laughed again in the afternoon when we all reloaded for the long ride home, I learned to always stay alert on the bus. I don't recall now how many tricks were played during the year, but I expect there were a lot. Even though he never laughed or said anything, I imagined Mr. Williams had a sense of humor and told his family about it around the supper table. He couldn't have expressed it to us. If he had opened that door, he would've lost control.

My Rat War

for Phillip and Brad

When we moved into the ranch house rental by the creek, I was glad to get to know Gary at work and call him a friend. He'd told me: "Ya'll be careful of snakes and rats if the water comes up in your yard." I didn't believe him and laughed. After all, the house was built up about two and a half feet off the ground, and even though the garage was ground level, I didn't think we had anything to worry about. While I was watching TV and my wife was reading in the bedroom, I heard crunching sounds in the wall of the kitchen and an inspection of the kitchen made me think I saw droppings behind the refrigerator.

I couldn't imagine setting traps that would smash a mouse and that I would have to clean up, so I bought the box kind with a glue floor. There in the box, they just stick and eventually die. My wife said it was cruel, that I would have to then kill them, but I told her I'd just throw the box and mouse in the trash outside. When the trash men took the bag to the dump, the mouse would be crushed. In the night, I heard a squealing sound and I imagined he was moving his head around and calling out---maybe to relatives and friends, maybe to me for relief. I quickly put the trap and mouse in a plastic grocery bag and tied it up and took it out to the can, and even when I tossed it in, I could hear the squeal.

The next day when I got home and opened the garage to pull the vehicle inside, I noticed something moving alongside the wall. I left the car running and jumped out to investigate. There, crouched in the corner, was a wharf rat, that seemed the size of a fully grown cat. I called my friend Gary to ask him what to do. I didn't have a gun, the rake I bought to clean elm leaves was plastic, and my extra glue trap would only fit one of his feet he was so big. I sprayed it with bleach and Windex and it stood up on its hind legs and hissed at me. I figured it was the parent of the little one I'd sent to the dump.

When my friend Gary got there, he said, "That ain't a wharf rat. It's just a rat."

"That's what we called them in Florida," I said.

Gary hit it on the head with a shovel and then scooped it up and tossed it out by the creek. "Buzzards'll get him," he said, spitting a stream of tobacco juice in my yard and shifting his plug of Red Man from one cheek to another. "You got to learn our rural mountain ways, boy."

"Well, we didn't have those things in the city."

"They in the city as well as in the country. Ya'll didn't live near the water?"

"No," I said. "Our town house was inland."

"Might better get you a gun. Don't let that little dog of yours go near the creek at night. Coyotes come off that mountain at night and drink."

I thanked Gary, and at night, I listen for the rats and the coyotes. Off in the distance, I have heard howling in the night, but I've never seen one. I'll keep checking, but I have dreams the rats have their own community in the walls and under the house. At night they invade and nibble on floor crumbs, food in the cupboard, and trash in the can. I dream they have declared war against me for killing their friends and relatives. I worry about us having a baby and the rats nibbling on the baby. I've seen stories on the news about that. Scout the terrier often whimpers from his kennel, but when I wake and go turn on the light to check, all is quiet and I don't see anything.

Sex Offender

When the Sheriff's department posted a link to the latest sex offender registry on FaceBook, I clicked just to see if any of the perverts lived near us. What I never expected to see was my Great Uncle Albert on the list. I immediately dialed my mother's number.

"Mom, Uncle Albert is on the sex offender's registry."

"I know; it's embarrassing."

"What'd he do?"

"He grabbed a big woman's behind in Wal-Mart and then groped her."

"Do you know why?" I imagined Uncle Albert in his mid-eighties, wisps of hairs on his mostly bald head, and humped over with crooked fingers from arthritis lunging forward toward a woman's behind on the cereal aisle in Wal-Mart.

"He's got Alzheimer's, bless his heart." She said it with a little inflexion and quiver, as if she was concerned she might have inherited the gene.

"I didn't know."

"Well, we have tried not to tell people, but now, we just have to tell. We don't want anyone thinking of Uncle Albert as a pervert hanging out in Wal-Mart."

"No, I'm sure you don't. Do you think he'll go to trial?"

"I don't know. We're likely going to have to put him in a home. My guess is they'll drop the charges."

"I hope so."

"He doesn't even know what he's doing half the time. He's just confused and frustrated. It's so sad. He wouldn't have wanted to live like this. His grandmother had it and wandered off in the winter and they found her a month later stiff as a board in a snow bank."

"Wow. You know, there was probably a time when he was younger he probably wanted to grab a woman's behind and didn't."

"Probably so. He was quite the lady's man when he was younger."

"Maybe the brain just switches to those impulses, thoughts, and dreams that weren't acted on, becoming more real than the part of the brain that doesn't work because the filters are off."

"Makes sense. I don't know. They say it's complicated."

"Let me know if I can help."

"Okay, thanks. Talk to you soon." After the call ended, I knew I couldn't help. I would if I could, but they needed special care that I couldn't provide, and with work, family, and community, there's simply not enough time. I shouldn't think it, but part of me felt Uncle Albert might be better off wandering off in the winter and being found in a snow drift, like his grandmother. Within a year, though, he died from a head injury in a nursing home after toppling over behind a nurse in the hallway.

The Tooth

My new year was off to a great start. I didn't make New Year's resolutions, but I simply made up my mind to make changes in my life. I have been on a "avoid sugar and bread" and "avoid snacking at night while watching television" diet. Seemingly, it was working, little by little. There was extra give in my pants, I didn't get as frightened when I caught a glimpse of myself in the mirror, and I didn't have problems breathing when I bent over to tie my shoes. Even my energy level and enthusiasm for life had returned.

As I was having my early morning coffee and eating some crisp bacon, and while watching the polar vortex on *The Weather Channel*, I felt the bacon crunch, and I slurped coffee to help wash it down. The crunch was different; it seemed even harder than when one bites down on an overly well done piece of the strip of bacon. Once the bacon was finished and once I finished my coffee, I was swirling my tongue around in my mouth and noticed I'd lost a portion of one of my back molars on the upper jaw.

Panic set in and my heart raced. I emailed my dentist's office and left a voice mail. I frantically began to do Google searches to see if I could digest a half molar, or if it would be sent to the appendix and would rupture. I tried to see the cracked tooth, but couldn't, and my wife saw it and said, "That just doesn't look good."

I realized this is the molar that was filled forty years ago, when I was a child. Though most of them had been filled, this was the largest filling. The procedure had taken the longest and sent me writhing in the dental chair to the point that I had been restrained by my mother and the red-headed dental assistant while the dentist drilled. Forty years later, I can still smell my molar being ground, the liquid silver being poured into my tooth, filling it and packing it tight. I can hear Dr. Minor, "There, now, it's gonna be all right. This won't take but a minute." His accent was old South, like Jimmy Carter's, where r's were not as pronounced and sound like "ah."

His own teeth, gold and silver, showed when he talked, and my instinct of reaching and searching for truth in his eyes was thwarted by the thick magnifying goggles he wore to get close up in my mouth. Even the candy and dime toys in the treasure chest didn't seem compensation enough to take away the fear. When I became a teen and my siblings had to get braces, I was silently thankful to Dr. Minor for telling me, "Just push on the back of your teeth at night and they'll straighten." The bottom teeth did straighten. There wasn't much to do about the discoloration because of the tetracycline I'd been given as a child, and through the years, I had to have more teeth filled. Even in college, the fillings began to crack and come out and they were all replaced, which was not all that fun, and even as a grown adult, I gripped the chair when they began to work in my mouth whether medicated or not.

Six months earlier, I'd been for a cleaning, and the dental hygienist didn't use the ultrasonic water pic to remove the plaque build-up; instead, she'd used the periodontal scaler, and as she approached my mouth, I imagined her to be a serial killer with a pickaxe. I closed my eyes and gripped the leather cushioning on the dental chair and for some unknown reason, my eyes even had tears. She asked if was okay, and I told her my allergies were really bothering me.

Saturday and Sunday, I didn't receive a call back or a returned email. I didn't have pain and chewed on one side, fearing the rest of the tooth would break apart, or the filling, which was still in place, would tumble out and fill the appendix if it couldn't be digested. I attended a children's basketball game for my son Saturday and was telling my friend Paul about the tooth incident. He looked at me, grinned, and said, "This too shall pass."

And pass it did. My dental office called first thing Monday morning and arranged for me to see the dentist after lunch. The shot to numb stung, but my hands were already gripping the chair. I eavesdropped on another patient's conversation in the bay next to mine. I could hear her rambling to the dentist about having these two pulled so her dentures could fit better. She told him she could get the rest of them pulled when she went back home to Dothan, compliments of the state. My mouth was numb and when I smiled into the pull down television, I could see my reflection on screen. I looked as if I had a stroke and my mouth was "drawn up." I then heard the patient next to me tell the doctor, "If it wasn't for my daughter, I'd still have all my teeth." Dr. Christoff said, "How's that?" "Yep, she sucked all the calcium right out of my teeth." I found myself laughing, drool landing on my clip-on bib.

A temporary crown followed by a permanent one was just the cure for the situation. I had been concerned about insurance, but it was covered. I certainly didn't want to pay for it. I wondered how my parents paid for their dental care along with mine and my three siblings, and I wondered how Dr. Minor made it, taking payments on credit from poor folks from all over the county. Life seemed more honest and simple then and while reflections were comforting, I hated what the tooth signified, namely that like Dr. Minor and my tooth, we will one day pass.

Oedipus

Rosalyn got to work early, wearing her turquoise custodial uniform with her name stitched on the left breast. Rarely did any of the faculty speak to her when they saw her pushing the dust mop across the tiled hallways, mopping restrooms, or cleaning toilets, except Professor Robinson.

Rosalyn wore comfort shoes, the same type some of the nursing faculty wore on the first floor. She always had less cleaning on the first floor compared to the second, where the Liberal Arts faculty were housed. "Tanto papel," she told her husband. Of course, there was a lot of paper because the faculty were writing and getting published, but she didn't understand promotion and tenure. Rosalyn, however, understood a great deal about the faculty and could have told administrators and her priest a lot: who was having relations and who smoked, drank, and took drugs in their offices.

Her routine before faculty arrived was to empty all trashcans, wipe their desks (if the desks were paper and book free, that is; she didn't like moving their things), and wipe their phones. Wiping phones wasn't required, but Rosalyn she saw it as her way of helping because of germs. She heard Robinson whimpering, but didn't dare check. Later, when she was in the hallway, Rosalyn heard a gunshot.

"Dios Mios!" Rosalyn screamed down the hallway, stairs, and to first floor, where one nurse came to her aid. Rosalyn had a difficult time translating into English when she was upset. "I think someone shot Professor Robinson." The nurse closed and locked her office door and called security. They held hands. Within minutes, campus and local police were searching the building for a shooter and breaking into Professor Robinson's office. The officer found her crumpled against the door, blood and brain matter splattered on the wall and floor. The pistol was still in her hand.

The note taped to her computer monitor revealed her dilemma and word traveled fast around the campus. "Dios Mio," Rosalyn said when her supervisor shared.

The Dean fired her because she hadn't received tenure. Her note also revealed she was ending her life because she couldn't live without her student lover. Due to a bizarre turn of events, she had discovered he was genetically her son. As an undergraduate, she'd donated eggs to a clinic in order to make extra money. Many of her friends had done it, and many of her male friends had donated sperm. The horrible thought came into her mind one morning when her student lover got out of bed and walked across the room. With his back facing her, she noted a birthmark on his shoulder blade identical to hers. She felt it too strange and had secretly collected saliva samples on Q-tips to send to a DNA company. When the results came many weeks later, her nightmare was confirmed. She left her belongings to her newly discovered son. He didn't understand, but was appreciative of the stuff.

Looney Tunes

We stood in the damp, cold December afternoon waiting for the Christmas parade and became excited at hearing the distant beating of drums and music from the high school band, the Tasmanian devil its mascot. We craned our necks to see them rounding the corner of Love and Church streets. Mayor Claghorn led the procession on its two-mile journey snaking through downtown. An overweight fellow, the Mayor wore a winter white suit, and wiped at his nostrils with a red silk scarf, in honor of the holidays, that matched his suit pocket square. Newly elected, Mayor Claghorn waved and smiled at the crowd while the Tasmanian Devils played *Camptown Races*. Each time, the horns played, "Do-dah, Do-dah," Mayor Claghorn did a little two-step and laughed at himself. Clearly, he enjoyed his new role.

One of our new neighbors standing next to us, who was uneducated, but had money and attitude, said, "He's not all that bright, but he'll do as he's told." I thought that a rather odd comment, but had already learned in our brief time in the small, deep South town, that she, along with many others, acted as if she knew more than everyone offering advice on politics and religion whether solicited or not. I wanted to hang "No Solicitation" signs around my house to keep her out of the yard, but I'm not sure she knew the meaning of the word and was probably too lazy to look it up, signified by her semi-tire behind. Her nails were always painted, one couldn't help but notice as she gesticulated, and her hair was dyed and curled.

After the Mayor and the Tasmanian Devils was a float from the local technical college, where anyone could take classes toward a certificate or technical degree free. I learned once they finished one, they could even switch to another program and get it free. It seemed a waste of taxpayers' money. The bipartisan idea behind it was educating the masses, building the workforce, but it had become a thing like the 1950s horror flick, *The Blob*, absorbing and growing into a massive bureaucracy for Georgia, mimicking George Wallace's sweet home Alabama. I recalled how much I had to pay out of pocket for my own college education. We certainly weren't wealthy, living in a poorly insulated wooden house with no air conditioning. The attic fan helped, pulling in every smell from wild honeysuckle to the spray of a passing skunk and enough dust to keep any allergy doctor in business for life. Nonetheless, I hadn't qualified for aid and couldn't track my Native American ancestry enough to get a scholarship.

Next was an antique aqua Thunderbird with the tax commissioner, a plump, bald short fellow. I'd met him when I picked up the car tags and paid Georgia's outrageous ad valorem tax and fees for our vehicles. We'd come from a state where everyone paid a flat rate, a seemingly simple notion. I'd shook his hand and wondered if he had a stutter or was simply nervous talking to me because I had ask so many questions about taxes: "G-g-g-g-good to m-m-m-meet ya." Not only was their car tax outrageous, their real estate tax was based on a forty percent assessment instead of the normal twenty, and each time a house sold, they rushed to reassess to increase revenue. To top it off, since an interstate ran through the town and there was a build-up of motels, they had a whopping tourism tax. Since there wasn't really anything to tour, I mused it was another way to increase revenue. I later learned the local board gave the money to each other's businesses disguised in such a fashion to support tourism. While it was all open records, the public didn't care. Apathy was the norm and had been since the time when small town mafia ran things.

Another car, which was a restored Trans Am like the one from *Smokey and the Bandit* featured the Longleaf Pine queen. The white girl's crystal crown and her sequined gown glistened in the winter sun, and her white gloves covered hands that waved in a back and forth motion almost like an automated mannequin. As she passed, a newer convertible held the Strawberry queen, a plump African American. Her crown, too, glistened as did the silk dress she wore. Following the queens was the local State Farm insurance company float, and candy was tossed into the streets. Unfortunately, their tosses aimed at other children and I held my daughter's hand and said, "There will be more. Don't run into the street." Horses followed with riders from a nearby farm, and another float from an African American Episcopal Church with a choir singing Christmas gospel songs, swaying, and clapping, and children tossing candy to the crowd. Truly beautiful, I found myself humming along with them. I wanted to get on their float or walk along with them. Their tosses, too, seemed to land in other areas, and my daughter pulled on my arm and said, "Daddy, don't they see me?" I told her not to worry about it, and for the first time, I noted the candy was all directed to the African American children. "You notice anything?" I asked my wife. "Yep," she said.

We stayed until the end, when Santa was riding in the back of a Ford truck with "Here Comes Santa Claus" playing, and we walked toward the courthouse where children could take pictures with Santa. We'd hoped to use it on our Christmas card and mused our Northern friends would enjoy seeing Santa without snow and surrounded by pine straw and green grass. I noted some of the crowd was leaving, probably running to Wal-Mart or what they called a mall, which was a group of stores loosely strung together. When we got to the courthouse square, I noted we were a minority. The majority of families were Hispanic migrant workers or African Americans. Christmas music was blaring, crackle mixed in the speaker system.

The mayor moved to the stage, standing askew from the podium. Another fellow, and much shorter, shuffled to the podium and pulled the microphone down toward his mouth. "May I have your attention please?" I hadn't seen this fellow around town, but he was plump, older, but had yellow hair. His voice was strange, childlike, and I learned from a lady standing next to me that his name was Mr. Skelton, the town manager. "He sweet, too," she said and laughed, her bobbing breasts making Martin Luther King's face on her shirt seemed contorted. Later, as we were standing in line, Mr. Skelton came up to me, extended his hand for a shake, but didn't grip. When he said, "Good to meet ya'll," it was a deeper voice and he offered a strange grin.

After being introduced, the mayor gripped the podium with one hand, waved at folks he likely couldn't see since the direction of his view and wave had no one waving at him, and said, "I say, it's good to see ya'll here. We're glad you people could come out today to celebrate the season, and we gone have some bar-be-cure available. 'Preciate all the workers here for winter pickin'. Ya'll vital to our town and we 'preciate ya'll paying your rent on time and in cash. I say, we hopin' ya'll have a Merry Christmas."

The winter vegetables were delicious, as were the spring and summer ones, and we adjusted to our new lives in a new South that was less new than the same South with a new coat of spray-paint.

Dog War

"No one should have to bury a child," is what my grandmother had said time and again after losing her own daughter at twelve to a mysterious infection that could have been cured today with antibiotics, and forty years later, after attending the funeral of my neighbor's son Isaac, I can still her saying it and couldn't agree more. Isaac wasn't even a relative, but my wife and I, now retired, enjoyed watching him through the bay window of our house across the cul-de-sac. He'd ride his bike up and down the street, his white-blonde hair blowing in the wind. We enjoyed watching him and his father play catch in the front yard. We enjoyed their annual collage photo Christmas card and note about what Isaac had done throughout the year in school, what belt he'd attained in taekwondo, what educational trips they'd taken during the summer, and we enjoyed talking to him when he'd come to sell items as part of the school, church, and Boy Scouts' fundraisers.

I knew the neighbors who lived diagonally from our house in the Chicago style bungalow were going to be trouble when they built the dog kennels out back of their house. Well, we'd even heard speculation at the Senior Center before they moved in he smoked marijuana and that she was a bully and gossip. Probably compensating for her own inadequacy, the typical uneducated, never been anywhere, small town type who hated outsiders, like me and my wife who retired here because of low taxes and a good climate. We'd even delivered a loaf of banana nut bread when they moved in. Never even got a thank-you note. Trash.

The husband who owned a plumbing company was an avid hog hunter and had multiple pit bulls, some of which I heard cost hundreds of dollars. Almost every other weekend, he would load some of those dogs into the kennels on the back of his plumbing truck and be gone until late

They had a chain link fence installed around the back yard, and once in a while I'd see the wife, a bubble-butt looking woman with dyed red-auburn hair who worked as a hairdresser, and their toddler, out back in the yard. Even those dogs would bark at them, and I knew if one of them dogs ever got lose, it would tear that poor toddler, and maybe her mama, to shreds. I'd heard enough stories through the years about those dogs. They've been bred for generations to hunt, to go for blood, and when they stay caged up and don't get to hunt, that tension builds in their system. They go crazy, like an addict needing another fix.

We were watching *Good Morning America* when I noticed Isaac riding his bike, and I didn't hear the screaming because of the crowd yelling and holding up their signs about where they were from, saying hello to friends and loved ones, on TV. When the show went to commercial, there was enough of an interlude that I heard the last of Isaac's screams. I didn't think about my knees and the pain. I just ran out the front door, grabbed a rock rake, and hurried as fast as I could to the street where Isaac was being yanked around on the asphalt by one of those pit bills like a rag doll. He was covered in blood and the jaws had a grip around his neck. I took the rake and plunged it into that dog. "You son-of-a-bitch! Let him go, you son-of-a-bitch!" The pit bull was whimpering and laying on its side as I continued to plunge the rake's steel teeth into his body, like he'd done to poor Isaac. "You fucking damned dog! That fat-ass hairdresser and her shit head husband. Fucking white trash. Somebody ought to tie them up and let their god-damned blood thirsty dogs have a go at them."

My wife had come to the door and called the ambulance. Isaac's father was at work, and his mother had never heard a thing. She had been listening to Christmas music and baking cookies. Who the hell felt like Christmas now, I wondered. My wife cried and cried. She'd never seen anything like it. Poor Isaac mauled to death by a pit bull and the trash neighbors had the gall to come to the funeral and the wife telling people they couldn't believe that one dog went mad, but the others were okay. Isaac's parents should have sued them, made them have all the damned dogs put to sleep, but they listed their house and said they were going to move and try to start a new life. Maybe have another child.

I don't believe they'll ever get over it. Just like my grandmother said. No amount of "It was his time," "Thank God for the time you had with him," and "God will take care of you" will get them through such an event. I won't either. I believe in God, but I don't understand how a God would allow such. I keep thinking about those damned neighbors and their hunting dogs. I might go over there when they are both at work and poison them one at a time, over time, so not to get caught.

It'd be a misdemeanor if I did get caught, but I don't need the trouble. Killing them off won't bring Isaac back, and it probably won't make me feel any better either, but at least no one else will have to fear an attack. I keep the rake in the bushes by the front door and now have a loaded pistol in the bombe chest in the foyer. I take it with me when I get the mail.

The Jog

Ben liked jogging late at night, his paper-white legs and glow-in-the-dark running shorts and shoes stood out in the glimmer of street lights. He knew the area was considered high crime, but he also knew where he could score some pot and was willing to take the risk. He knew habitual behaviors were often noticed by others, particularly criminals, so he scanned like a periscope as he ran.

As he rounded a corner on the sidewalk, two hooded black males jumped from behind an oak and grabbed him. One held him and put a gun to his head while the other reached in his running shorts and took the wallet, grabbed the cash, and threw the wallet on the ground. He couldn't hear their mumbles because of the i-pod speakers blaring R.E.M.'s "It's the End of the World as We Know It" and he then felt a tug on his shorts, hands grabbing his cheeks, being bent, and felt the violation by both, one after another. As quickly as it happened, they were gone, and Ben grabbed the wallet and stumbled back to his apartment where he showered and swore he'd never tell, he'd never jog there again, he'd block it from memory, and he'd quit scoring pot from that area of town.

Flashes come to mind when the sky goes dark and he's driving through town and sees young hooded guys or when he's in the grocery store and makes eye contact. He swears they smile at him and he doesn't leave the grocery store until he sees them drive away. He wants to follow them and kill them with his new pistol he keeps in the glove compartment, but he needs to make sure. He'd hate to make a mistake.

Hokey Pokey

Ray Anthony's mama had been after him to change---quit smoking and drinking and frequenting Ms. Greer's piano bar downtown. She didn't know about the marijuana and sex.

"Need to get it together before it's too late," she said. "I'd like to see your sorry ass in heaven. I'd hate for you to go to hell with all them Muslims and other heathens."

"You reckon they let you talk like that up there?"

"Damned right they will, if you're saved. That's what matters."

Ray Anthony knew he needed to change. He was always coughing up phlegm and it was nasty. He also knew the hard liquor he knocked back at Ms. Greer's made him crazy. There were nights he'd gone home with others, smoked pot, woke up in strange places, and knew he'd sinned. He knew the fun-filled feelings were temporary and meaningless, when he remembered them.

He knew Jesus lasted a lifetime. He'd seen his mama change when he was a young boy--her own smoking and drinking turned to getting saved and dragging him to church every time they opened the doors. She'd dance around the living room while cleaning and sing gospel songs, holding a white handkerchief just like Vestal Goodman. For ten year old Ray Anthony, it was a site to behold. He felt like she was an angel; she certainly had the voice of one.

On Sunday, Ray Anthony went to church with his mama for the first time in many years, went down the aisle and got saved. A week later he was baptized and the following week, his mama was diagnosed with terminal pancreatic cancer, stage four. They gave her two months.

Ray Anthony was glad his mama got to see him turn himself around, and when he buried her, he decided to give up painting houses and go after a more stable job with the government. After testing, he finally landed a job delivering mail for the U.S. Postal Service. When he's running short on delivery time, he takes the mail home and piles it up in his spare bedroom. He wants to be on time and stay in good with the government. He believes what they don't know won't hurt them or him. Plus, it's mostly junk mail. He tries to sort through it and deliver what he thinks might be important the next day.

Most days, after he has sorted mail and eaten supper, Ray Anthony sits in a chair in the living room, listening to old gospel music. Sometimes he imagines his mama cleaning, humming, holding her white handkerchief, and turning herself around and around.

Mud Island Monorail

Poplar Avenue came to a dead-end at Front Street in Memphis, and the parking lot was the last concrete to be seen before the mighty Mississippi. After paying the six-dollar fee, we parked and walked in, purchasing tickets. We took the escalator up to the third floor to board the monorail. The red monorail reminded me of the one at Disney, moving quickly across land and a portion of the river to Mud Island, a river park with a first class museum, where tourists can learn about the history of the river--the battles fought, the ecological life, the influence on culture from blues and rock and roll to great literature.

As I glanced out the window, I noted that once the monorail left the concrete boarding station, there didn't seem to be any tracks. My heart thumped and I turned to the guide and asked if it was suspended.

"Nah. Goes right out there," she said.

"Yes," I said. "But where is the track?"

She pointed up, and I looked out about the time the doors closed with a swoosh and locked tight. I sat down and gripped the metal pole. "Oh my God," I said to myself. I felt dizzy and looked only at the floor, taking deep breaths. It only took a few minutes before it stopped and the doors opened.

"You okay?" my wife asked.

"Of course, I am. Just tired."

"Well, I'm surprised you rode this. We're pretty high up and I know you don't like heights."

"It's not that high up, three or four stories. It's just hanging there, suspended, though, not like the one at Disney World or even the Marta in Atlanta."

She laughed. "Come on."

After enjoying the museum and taking photos of great river vistas, the metal "M" shape over the I-40 bridge between Arkansas and Tennessee, and tug boats and barges, we walked the scale model and were impressed with the marker locations of cities and towns along the river that gave facts about the river. It felt good removing our shoes and dipping our feet into the cool waters. After a couple of hours, we decided to find the Peabody, check in to our room, watch the infamous ducks march, and enjoy some blues and barbecue on Beale Street.

I told my wife maybe we should just walk back. If the monorail were supported by a bridge or tracks, I wouldn't like it, but I'd feel better. I felt like this monorail was on a hanging zip line, something I'd never try. "Oh, come on, it'll be fine. Plus, I'm getting tired and would prefer not to walk the bridge."

"Okay." On the monorail, there was an elderly couple, a mother and two children, and an employee I remembered from the gift shop. As the monorail left the deck, there was a slight dip, followed by a loud pop. I gripped the pole, and then watched a portion of the car come unattached and move down dangling. Our portion was still connected, but I felt it was a matter of time.

"Everyone move to this end," I yelled, and amid the sudden crying and praying, they listened. I already had 911 on my phone and explained to the dispatcher. Apparently, there were other calls, too.

"Sir, is everyone in the car all right?"

"I think so. Just scared."

"Help is on the way," she said, but I didn't feel reassured how a rescue might happen midair with the monorail dangling over a portion of the Mississippi. The guide did not have life preservers and didn't know what to do. She kept texting and wiping tears. A flurry of onlookers over at Mud Island and then back at Front St. gathered, cupping hands to block the sun so they could watch our disaster unfold. I kept looking in both directions for a boat that would throw out a self-inflating raft, but the only thing I saw were firemen, police officers, and emergency medical technicians running on the bridge above that seemed to create a vibration I didn't think was good for our situation. Next, ropes and pulleys were lowered and instructions were yelled through a bullhorn: "Women and children first."

Since the doors would not open, I kicked out the window. It was large enough to get everyone through without discomfort. The mother and her two children were first, followed by my wife and the elderly woman. The guide and gift shop worker were next.

The elderly man said, "Son, I just don't know if I can do this. I didn't want to ride this damned thing to begin with."

"Me neither," I said. "This thing's not going to hold much longer. Let's just do it."

I hooked him up, pushed him out and they pulled him up. As I hooked myself up and shoved off, the monorail crashed into the river below, and I hung there a moment, like a catfish on a line a fisherman forgot to reel, hearing screams, followed by, "I think I've got him," and was pulled to the bridge. I didn't want to stand. I wanted to stay curled in a fetal position on the concrete, but I knew the bridge was one quake away from plummeting into the mighty Mississippi below with movement from the New Madrid seismic zone.

"You okay?" my wife asked.

"I told you we shouldn't have ridden that thing."

"Well, we won't next time."

In the hustle and bustle that included kids telling their dad via cell phone how cool it all was and the elderly couple calling their children before it made the nightly news, I forgot to thank the rescue workers for helping and thought I would send an email later.

The Cleaners

Her tights had Marilyn Monroe faces, she wore a figure-hugging T-shirt, and her hair was a purple weave. She was a remarkable sight at the cleaner's drive-thru.

When the window slid open, she asked, "You picking up?"

I nodded, and she turned to gather the cleaned and pressed clothes draped in plastic. I glanced at the garments she hung on a rod by the register while she scanned tickets. "That shirt ain't mine," I said.

"It's got your name on it," she said.

I looked closer. My glasses had smudge marks. Maybe it was my wife's shirt or my son's. I handed her the next bundle to be cleaned. "These shirts just need pressing. They're already clean." I had found washing them in advance, and just having the cleaners press, was one way of saving money.

"Alright."

"Thanks," I said.

"Uh-huh," she said, turning and sliding the window closed.

I had to overlook the language, in addition to the inappropriate business-attire, since they were the only cleaners in town. I hung the clothes on the grab handle in the ceiling of the car and closed the back door.

When I got home, I went through the clothes. The yellow shirt I didn't think was mine seemed new and was a size too small for me. It didn't belong to my wife or son either. I was mad – mad that they were wrong and wouldn't admit it, mad at myself for not being more assertive, mad at paying for something I shouldn't have.

Rather than give it back, I folded it neatly with tissue paper, wrapped it and gave it to my brother for his birthday; it was his size. When I told him the story, he laughed and said, "Well, that doesn't make up for the pants of mine they lost, but it helps."

Car Wash

The winter had been tough; not many days made it above freezing and the mountains and clouds kept what little sunshine to themselves. The snow and salt changed my blue SUV to a grayish white up to the door handles, and I had heard that combination could be hard on paint. I tried to spray the SUV using the garden hose in the flowerbed, but the cheap plastic nozzle had cracked and leaked on my hands. I ran into the garage, got the gardening gloves, and tried again. As I sprayed, the snow and salt stayed on the car and very little dirt came off. Instead, what looked like small icicles began to form on the bottom of the car and I gave up. I tossed the gardening gloves on the sink in the garage to dry and left for work.

I hadn't watched the news or weather, but when the radio disk jockey said we'd see the sun and the temperature would get above freezing, I vowed to visit the car wash during lunch. After eating my sandwich at my desk, I left the office. The line was unusually long, but I waited. There was a hint of spring in the air, just enough to entice the gullible into believing, but I was a realist and didn't put faith in the disk jockey's report.

Once I fed my debit card to the machine and the automated voice told me I could proceed, I gauged where the tires fit into the tracks and moved forward. I could hear the rubber squeaking against the metal and when the red light appeared, I stopped on cue. I didn't feel comfortable putting the SUV in neutral, taking my foot off the break, releasing my grip on the steering wheel.

First came the soap. The metal dispensers shot blue and orange soap all over the SUV and when it got to the back, it turned sideways and spayed. Fully soaped, I waited and noted the antenna that I forgot to take off. I had heard others complain the giant spinning brushes could snap them in two, and as the brushes began spinning on the front and sides, I cringed and knew it was too late. I never saw or heard the antenna break off, but once the brushes left that area, I heard a repeated scraping sound and realized the metal antenna had somehow become stuck in the brush and was scraping the windshield. Then it moved in the brush to the roof. The metal wedged in the crack between my roof and sunroof. All of the spinning brushes locked in place and I smelled burning and noted smoke behind an aluminum panel of the apparatus on the wall. I also noted paint flecks dripping down on my windshield. I blew my horn and imagined the car wash was destroying my SUV. Visions of the blob from an old movie that devoured anything in its path became even more real.

It seemed like a long time, but I think it was only a couple of minutes before the attendant cut the power. The spinners halted, but I could not exit the vehicle until he manually moved them. I drove over the tire hold and out into the parking lot. I got out and saw the paint on the sides and roof had been worn down in places from repeated spin of the bristles and my windshield was cracked. Only a portion of my antenna remained, but it was enough for me to hear the disk jockey declare an early spring and a beautiful day.

"Man, what the hell? I ain't ever seen anything like it," the car wash attendant said.

"Me neither. This is awful."

"You want the owners name and number?"

"Yeah. I know I'll need a police report for insurance." I pressed 911 on my cell. Even though I knew it wasn't an emergency, it was probably the most action the town had seen all week. The officer took all of the relevant details and gave me a copy. I stopped by my insurance agent's office on my way back to work, and the office staff came outside to see the damage. They promised they would expedite the claim and send it to the home office and that a claims representative would be in touch.

Back at my office, my co-workers came out to see the damage. The front end, hood, and the body up to the front doors were clean. The side passenger doors to the back end of the vehicle still contained salt and snow and remained a gray color, except for the dried blue and orange soap. I felt the car was totaled and I thought about what sort of SUV I might get. The next day at lunch, I drove by dealerships to see if there were any SUVs that appealed to me.

After work a couple of days later, I checked my voice mail at home. First was a message from the car wash owner, extending his apologies. He also suggested that as the sign noted, I should have removed the antenna. He commented he'd contact my insurance company for damages to the car wash. I was astounded. The second message was from my insurance company. The claims representative said that I had been at fault and was not eligible for coverage. I did not place the phone back on its cradle. I threw it across the living room, smashing it into pieces.

That night, I dreamed I was stuck in the car wash and the equipment caved in on and around my SUV, pushing me through the metal grate into the drain below. When I awoke, my heart was fluttering and my t-shirt was soaked with sweat. I turned over and wondered if I would have to take a second job to pay the damages and get another SUV.

Losing My Religion

People said that when I turned fifty, I would fall apart, but I laughed and thought they were crazy. A couple of weeks ago, I attempted to reach clothes in the washer, pull them out, and bend to put them in the drier. I twisted, something pulled in my lower back, and I froze. It took a minute before I worked up the nerve to move, and I walked stooped from the laundry to the cabinets in the kitchen. My hands gripped the granite counter tops, and I slowly pulled myself back into a vertical position. The pain in the lower back continued and felt like someone had stabbed me with a knife and then twisted it around. "Son of a…," I said.

I made it to the bedroom. The Ethan Allen cherry bed was too high for me to jump on, so I used the matching step stool and planted both feet on the first step. Before the next step, I extended my arms perpendicular and gripped the bed's posts for balance. I placed me knees first and then toppled over and crawled like a baby. It hurt to lay on my stomach or my back and I managed to turn to my side. "Son of a…" I refrained from the rest and my son walked in.

"Dad, I can hear you."

"Sorry." I don't know how many times I'd told him cursing at everything was inappropriate. "Where's your mom?"

"She's walking the dog."

"Go get her."

"What's wrong? Are you okay?"

"No, I hurt my back. I need to go to a doctor. Bring my iPad and my phone."

He was quick. "Here they are."

"Thanks, buddy. Now go get your mom."

While Sam went to look for Melissa, I did a Google search on my iPad for back doctors. I knew it had to be skeletal or muscle related, but I had never had this and had never felt such pain. I had heard my mother, my wife's mother, grandparents, and others complain about back related issues for years and over time, I tuned them out, wasn't empathetic in any way. In fact, I wondered if they didn't whine about it to justify their desire for pain pills. "I'm sorry," I said to an empty room. "I take back the eye-rolls, the curses under my breath, the thinking you all were just lazy asses." I half-hoped my repentance might ease the pain, but it didn't. I knew it was illogical, but at that point, anything was worth a shot.

The search revealed two choices: a chiropractor or an orthopedic surgeon. I knew folks who had been to both, so I figured who ever I reached first was the one I'd see. I left a message for the chiropractor and they called me back and said they could work me in first thing. The orthopedic office didn't have voice mail. They had an answering service, but the service directed me to call back. For an emergency, they advised visiting the emergency room, something I didn't want to do because of the wait and the possibility I might catch something else since everyone in town who had the flu or virus was hanging out in there, coughing and spraying their germs all over the place.

Melissa helped me into her car. At least it wasn't my SUV, which was higher and had step rails. When we arrived in the parking lot, she pulled to the door, to lessen my walking distance. I fell over onto the sidewalk. "Son of a…"

"Watch your mouth," she said.

"Damn it, I'm sorry, but it hurts."

"Others might hear you."

She helped me up and I hobbled inside. Forms needed completing and they needed copies of my driver's license and insurance cards. Most of the lines on the forms I had problems seeing. The month before, the eye doctor had suggested I get bifocals, but I said I didn't need them.

X-rays and consult complete, the chiropractor dressed in blue scrubs showed me trauma on vertebrae: maybe wrecks, maybe the time I flipped off a friend's trampoline and landed on my back and couldn't breathe for a minute, maybe a bicycle accident (though landing on the bar likely injured other areas) maybe a football injury in middle school (though splinters lodged in butt cheeks from bench sitting might be a more appropriate injury), or maybe trauma from car wrecks as a teen. Between the trauma, bone spurs, and strained muscles, I needed therapy. I was, however, relieved not to have a tumor pressing on the spine or any other extreme scenario I had conjured. The chiropractor helped me to a table that moved and shifted, and I heard parts of my back snap, crackle and pop, louder than the cereal did when I ate it as a child. Then, a blonde assistant with perfectly white teeth came in and placed electrodes on my back and shoulders. When she turned on the machine, I felt the massage from electricity being fired into muscles. Between the massage and Native American flute music, I almost fell asleep. When the session was over, I asked for more. She assured I would need more treatments and I knew that meant more co-pays.

By the next day, the pain was only in spurts, when I turned a certain way or when I tried to bend over. I complained to Melissa that for once she needed to put the toilet seat up because I couldn't bend to put it up. I also couldn't wash my feet. I squirted liquid soap on my feet in the shower and rubbed them together and then rinsed. I didn't wear socks for two days and only wore slip on loafers. By Monday, Melissa had to put my socks on for work. I managed to drive my SUV, but I had to hoist myself in, using my arm muscles and I had to adjust the seat. Other than Tylenol, I hadn't taken any other medication. I used ice packs and some muscle rub samples from the chiropractor.

After a few days, I realized that I'm not very tolerant of pain and I do not like others assisting me. I also realized I don't like comments from friends on FaceBook who wrote to me that getting old isn't for sissies. I felt like we were in fifth grade again and I unfriended them and hope they'll turn a certain way, so they can feel back pain and lose their religion, too. The only good news was my two teenagers apparently felt enough empathy for me that they came, and checked on me, and had conversations with me, making the pain all somehow worth it.

Wet Nurse

I was a pall bearer at my Uncle Harry's funeral and felt torn. On the one hand, I hated it--hated that he'd died, hated what my cousins and aunt were going through--but I wanted to honor my dad's request to be a pall bearer and honor Uncle Harry. I respected the way he lived his life, working at the mill and running his family farm on the side with chickens, goats, cows and a pond stocked full with bream and catfish. I'd been a city boy and was always captivated by the quiet, the oddness of rural life. I'd even seen my uncle shoot a snake out of a tree. My grandparents, dead now for almost thirty years, had five children and he was the second to pass. His sister Doris who'd died as a child from pneumonia had been the first in the family to go, then my grandparents, and now Uncle Harry. It was hard to remember my grandparents; memories of them were fragmented, like flashes in a dream.

After the graveside service, we gathered at the church for a meal. An elderly woman came up to me and said, "Oh how I loved your grandmother."

I nodded. "Yes ma'am. We do miss her."

"She saved my life when I was a baby and many others, too."

"How's that?" I knew my grandmother didn't drive, didn't work outside the home.

"She was a wet nurse. Nursed me and kept me alive when my own mama couldn't."

"I had no idea." I imagined my grandmother in a rocking chair on her front porch suckling babies, a strange vision.

"I'm sorry about your uncle."

"Thank you," I said, and the older woman teetered off to the desert table. My wife smiled and I told her I didn't know about that. Later, I saw my aunt Barbara Jean cutting a slither of pecan pie. She bent over the desert table, her bones giving shape to thin skin as she cut the pie with the precision of a physician.

"Aunt Barbara Jean, that's not a big enough piece."

"I know, but I've got to keep my blood sugar in check."

"Was Granny a wet nurse?"

"Apparently so, but that was when I was young. I don't recall details, but she kept babies for extra money, and I guess it helped keep food on our table when Daddy got sick."

"I never knew it."

"Speaking of babies, you remember her bad leg?"

If my grandmother had been a man, she would've been a linebacker on a football team. She was broad, but had thin legs from the knees down. "I vaguely remember her having an issue with her leg. Mostly because of the old photos I've seen where she has it wrapped."

"Know what finally healed that ulcer on her leg?"

"What?" I expected aloe or some herbal concoction given she had plants for medicinal purposes all over her front porch.

"After birth. She called old Dr. Clement who was in his eighties then. He told me to come down to the hospital. He had wrapped a glob of it in a bag, told me to slice it and wrap it around her ulcerated leg in a poultice, changing it every other day for a week. End of the week came, and it healed from the inside out."

"After birth? That sounds disgusting."

"Don't be silly. Some cultures make soup with it. Animals eat it. You ought to see the dogs at your Uncle Harry's. Bought killed each other to get that after birth from a cow."

The city boy in me winced. "Well, it does make some scientific sense given the nutrients during pregnancy."

"Sure it does. I had them save mine from my kids and kept it in the freezer for years, right next to where I kept the hamburger meat. Used it when they got burned or had cuts. Didn't need no doctor, no medicine."

"Amazing," I said, and changing the subject, "You doing okay?"

"I'll be alright. We're all going to the tunnel at some point. Glad I'll know a few folks when I get there."

"Me, too." I wanted to tell my dad about the wet nurse and the after birth to get his reaction, to see what he knew, but decided to wait until later. It occurred to me just how much in the world had changed. No one heard of wet nurses much anymore and I'd never heard of a physician prescribing after birth as treatment. If this worked and helped society then, though, I figured it might come back around, like everything else.

Angler's Prayer

My grandmother had an old sign hanging from a rusty nail in the living room on the clapboard wall that read, "Lord give me the grace to catch a fish so big that even I, when telling of it afterward, may never need to lie". The sign hung next to a picture of Jesus right by a fireplace that had been sealed off. My grandmother fished, mainly using a cane pole cut, dried, and fashioned from reeds on my uncle's farm. My grandfather, too, fished, and in fact everyone in our family fished at some point. In fact, you might've been considered "off" or "not quite right" if you didn't. In Southern Georgia, people fished in ponds, rivers, or lakes with water that looked like dark tea and they were constantly scanning for moccasins.

When I was standing in the Davidson River in the Pisgah National Forest near Brevard, North Carolina, on a day when the mist floated on the river, I thought about my family who would have enjoyed this----the coolness, the lack of gnats, clear water rushing over rocks, and bite after bite by beautiful rainbow trout. They would've loved the overhanging Rhododendrons in bloom until their carefully tied flies got hung.

What they wouldn't have loved is that I hired guides to assist us, not because we couldn't do it on our own, but because I didn't have the equipment or garb needed---socks, waders, fly rods, flies, nets, and because I didn't know much about fly fishing. I've been behind a desk for twenty years, not fishing in a river. What they would have hated most is the concept of catch and release. In fact, I could hear my grandmother saying, "I don't believe in that," just like she'd said about the moon landing. It's not that she denied reality so much as it was something that wasn't practical in her world. The point to them would be to catch, clean, fry, and eat them. The point to me was to get out of the office, turn off the devices, spend quality time together doing something we've never done, learn new things, and enjoy one of the most beautiful areas of the South. What my grandparents would have also thought absurd was not keeping up with how many we caught. At the end of our time, the guides thought we caught seventeen. To us, it didn't matter. We had no need to lie, to talk about the ones that got away, to talk about who caught the most or the biggest. We simply hated to leave the river and now, back in the world with all of our devices, we long to return.

Whistler

My grandfather was a carpenter, but he was also a whistler and the two went hand-in-hand. You couldn't find him working---sawing, shaving wood, nailing lumber--without whistling. There was a time I wanted to be like him, to be a carpenter and a whistler, but neither came easy to me. Every time he handed me a hammer, I slammed fingernails that turned blue and eventually came off, but always grew back. He didn't let me handle the electric saw. He showed me how to whistle, and I followed his lead and pursed my lips and formed an "O" like he directed, blowing in and out; there was a slight whisper that sounded more like a damaged metal pea whistle. He told me to keep practicing.

Mostly, I stayed inside and watched television shows with my grandmother: *Hazel, Bewitched,* and *The Beverly Hillbillies*. After a hot lunch, I'd take a nap and they continued to work: him outside in the heat of his shop and her inside with window units blowing ice cold air, electric fans on the floor circulating it. In the evening, my mom or dad got off work and collected me to go home. By then, my grandfather was wearing only a t-shirt, drinking Schlitz from a brown glass bottle, smoking a cigar, and watching the evening news: scenes of fighting and death in Viet Nam, peace signs from Nixon, hippies being arrested in California, or blacks being hosed in the South were stark contrasts from the day-time TV shows.

I continued to practice my whistling every day of the summer and when fall came and school was back in session, I heard a whistler even better than my grandfather. Our principal in elementary school brought in a famous whistler who entertained us with "The Fishing Hole," the theme song to *The Andy Griffith Show* along with other songs and even bird calls. After, the hallways echoed with kids from kindergarten through sixth making all sorts of whistling sounds. I'm sure the teachers enjoyed the echoes of whistles, as did our parents when we all got home, but none of them ever said anything negative.

As winter approached, my own whistling had improved and my grandfather told me it sounded good for a city boy, but once mastered, I had moved on to other things of childhood and teenage years: riding bikes, playing sports, and eventually working my first job in a restaurant cleaning tables and washing dishes. For twenty-five years, I didn't whistle, until my son skipped up to me asking me how after watching a cartoon. My long planted grandfather became more real than he was in my distant memories, and I quoted his instructions word for word. He hadn't changed the world when he was in it--neither had I, and in fact, most don't, but the whistling helped us feel better about it for a time.

The Brand

Pledging Kappa Omega fraternity was one of the best decisions I made my first semester at the college. Instantly, I had a circle of friends who would do anything for me, including give me copies of exams from the filing cabinet in the frat house for all of the classes and professors I had, but being a pledge meant doing things: carrying the books of one of the big brothers, cleaning up the vomit from frat parties, and working in the yard.

For a small town guy moving to a private college in the city made the transition easy. The campus look sold me---historical Jeffersonian brick buildings with a quad full of ancient trees creating a canopy effect. I was excited about being away from my parents in a city with restaurants and bars. Anytime I felt the need to see family, I could drive an hour and a half and have that need met, but my brothers kept me busy enough and became like family, decreasing my desire to go home.

The brothers were animated the week leading up to the formal initiation ceremonies at the KO house. My big brother Tim kept jabbing me in the ribs and asking me if I was excited. I was more afraid than anything because I had heard rumors of sex with sheep, conjuring ghosts of historic and famous fraternal brothers, and torture and whippings, but Tim just told me it was a lot of hype.

When Friday arrived and once the sun had gone down, we were blindfolded and led into the basement. I was second in a line of seven pledges. I heard a lot of whispering, doors closing, and moaning. Then someone told us to drop our pants and underwear. I did but kept my hands covering my genitals. I could hear my heart beat in my ears and my breathing was quick. Finally, the screams and cries of the first pledge in line Robert came from a different room and made my knees wobbly. I knew that whatever Robert was going through was coming for me next. I was lead into another room and lifted onto a cold table by brothers. Several of them began to hold me down while one or more began to fondle and slap my butt cheeks. I feared rape.

A cold liquid was wiped over my right cheek, and the brothers pressed further down on my body. Then, a hot substance began to press on my right cheek and burned until I screamed out and a hand rested on my left check. I didn't wail or blubber, but tears fell from my blindfold and even after the object was removed, my cheek continued to burn. Someone's hand rubbed some liquid onto the cheek. The brothers released their hold and picked me up. I was lead back into the room and given a robe to put on.

For a week, my butt hurt. I learned the brand had been hand forged by one of the brother's uncle who owned a large cattle farm. I also had to learn to wear my wallet in my left pants pocket, and I tried to avoid driving. By week two, the pain was almost gone and I enjoyed looking at my butt in the mirror after a shower and seeing the Greek Omega letter on my cheek. I never offered to be the brander in the fraternity or serve in any initiation ceremony. I just didn't believe I could do it. I'm not sure I would have gone through with the branding ceremony had I been given a choice, and I didn't like one of the brothers fondling and slapping my cheeks prior to the branding. I often wondered who that was, but I never had any indication.

Now when I look into the mirror, the Greek Omega has flattened and stretched to the point that it resembles a bad Botox lip job, and I wonder what my doctor and nurses will think when I go for a colonoscopy, if they even look.

The Reviewer

Exasperated from cleaning up after her teens and her husband Ron, Jennie settled in the den in a used mocha leather chair from Pottery Barn a writer had offered her after she'd written a glowing review for his fantastic sports melodrama published by one of the medium houses in the northeast. A plot-driven narrative, the novel had lots of potential in sales, and while there had been lots of alcohol and sex swaps, it was the use of steroids that had driven the story to a happy ending with a positive finding from a review board. For many, the story might have even been classified as a fantasy because of the positive finding and because the media had sided with the football player.

Jennie sipped her wine and glanced at her bookcase, full of free novels and story collections from big houses to self-published authors, and she had long since quit counting the reviews she'd churned out. She'd actually written enough reviews that she could have written a novel herself, but that wasn't going to happen. She wouldn't know where to start and didn't have a creative bone in her body. If it weren't for the dictionary and thesaurus, she couldn't have even written a review. She'd circle names and underline parts she thought were particularly good. Jennie had the formula, the same format she used for all her reviews, down pat, and she mostly plugged in basic info about the narrative, characters, and if she really liked the author, she'd throw in a comparison to a historical figure or maybe a big name. She had to run Google searches, so no one would know she hadn't read the historical writers, especially if it was a literary writer she couldn't understand if she tried.

"What're you doing?" Ron asked.

"Sipping some wine and getting in the mood for another read," Jennie said.

"What's next?"

"Chick lit novel by a writer named Marianne I met at a festival in the mountains."

"She a lesbian?"

"I don't know," Jennie said. "What does that matter?"

"There was something on the news about some lesbian writer whose book was going to be a movie."

"What book? Who was the author?"

"I don't know. I didn't pay attention."

"If they replay, let me know. I doubt it's Marianne. That doesn't sound like her or her writing."

"How many people read those reviews you write?"

"I don't know, but the writers like them. I like to think it helps them with their sales, too."

"But can't anyone write a review for those book sites? You don't have to be a reviewer, right?"

"Well, that's true. You could post one on Amazon, Goodreads, FaceBook or even Twitter. Probably other places, too."

"Couldn't I post something even if I hadn't read the book? Just make it up?"

"Well, I guess you could."

"What do you get out of it? You don't get paid."

"Well, I guess I enjoy the friendships I make."

"Friends? The only time you see or hear from these people is when you're writing a review, except for that woman who gave you the chair, or you meet up with them at one of those festivals you're always going to and what do they do? Sit around and talk about what they've done to a group of people who either want to be like them or rub elbows with them? They don't even pay your way there."

"Why are you being negative? Are you jealous, Ron?"

"I'm not being negative. I'm being realistic. I'm certainly not jealous of pretend, but I would like to understand it better. It's like kids I knew who had imaginary friends. I thought that was crazy even as a kid. Maybe I'll go with you to the next one."

"Okay, that would be awkward, but yeah, you can go, if you want to hang with the women writers."

"Would I have to read those books?"

"It might be helpful, unless you want to just sit at a gathering or dinner like a bump on a log."

"How do you think they would react to me? Think they'd pal up to me, hoping I might influence you to do more. I'll bet they wouldn't be mean to me even if I was ugly to them for fear you might write a bad review."

"Oh for goodness sakes, Ron. That's nuts."

"Is it? You've got a power that you buy. It takes you out of our house, away from me and the kids, and it makes you feel more special than you do in your job as a customer service agent in your cube for the auto parts company, and have you ever written a negative review?"

Ron walked away and under her breath, Jennie mumbled, "That son of a bitch." She knocked the wine back, emptying the glass, and got up to go to the kitchen for another. She looked around--the scarred Formica counter tops she wanted to replace with granite when they had the money, the grinding refrigerator with rust around the bottom, the popcorn ceiling sporting a wagon wheel light with orange glass. Jennie poured another glass full, walked back to the chair, plopped, and picked up the preview copy of Marianne's newest. She sipped the wine and found herself at the beach next to a life guard sporting red shorts. She imagined she might attempt a drowning, so she could be saved.

Oldies Concert

I bought a VIP ticket to the radio station's annual oldies concert at the city auditorium, so I got an early admission to the meet and greet with the singers from The Lovin Spoonful, The Drifters, The Association, The Turtles, and The Hollies. The only way the line-up could have been better was if the remaining Bee Gees showed. I brought my old albums for autographs in a double-bagged plastic Kroger bag and cleaned my cell screen for selfies.

The line wasn't as long as I had assumed, and I wrongly assumed the crowd might be mid-forties like me. They seemed much older, maybe mid-seventies, and I remembered it was my mom who had conditioned me to love this music when I was a kid in the late 1960s. She taught me and my siblings to dance, twisting to Chubby Checker across our wooden floors in a new brick home in the suburbs. My anticipation and excitement decreased, however, as I heard the comments from those in front and behind me in line: "I hope it gets out by 9:00. I need to take my medication", "I heard those auditorium seats aren't good for your back", and "They said one of the singers died last week and ain't coming, but I bet they won't give us a partial refund".

When the doors finally opened, I made my way to the stage area, where the singers sat behind folding tables poised for photos and autographs. As I stood in a line to meet the Yester brothers, one who had been a lead singer for The Association and one who had been a lead singer for The Lovin Spoonful, I noticed the lady in front of me. She was wearing jeans and a rhinestone shirt and cowboy boots. She turned and smiled at me, revealing two canine teeth (cuspids) on the top row of her mouth and was missing the four inscisors or front teeth between the canines. She looked like a vampire and maybe that was the look she was going for, but she turned to me and said, "That ugly guy in front of me just farted."

I laughed because I didn't think she thought she was ugly and because I couldn't believe she'd revealed that information to a complete stranger. "Oh no," I said.

When she stepped away, I shook the Yesters' hands, told them how much I had admired their music through the years, took a selfie, had my albums autographed, and moved on to the next line. I didn't see the vampire again, nor the fellow who farted. I found my seat and absorbed the oldies music, one hit after another, closed my eyes and imagined me and mom dancing on the wooden floors again.

Merger

When news that the two plants would merge was announced, I grimaced, shook my head and could only imagine what those I would leave behind were thinking. I knew folks were forwarding the email, running around to see who knew, and all of them were offering opinions. The result was a flurry of randomness, like a busy FaceBook feed---some turning to God and prayer, some biting each other's heads off like political ads, some throwing back to better times, some resorting to jokes and humor, some blaming others along class lines within the companies.

I'd been one of the fortunate few who'd landed a better job in another state before the merger was announced, my resume highlighting accomplishments in chronological order. The many times I had reviewed it, I would've hired me, too, for I felt I'd highlighted our best accomplishments. I'd read the body language of executives, picked up bits and pieces in speeches about efficiency, and like an animal sensing the earthquake, I turned those Darwinian survival skills into a plan to act, to move to safer and higher ground before the merger.

Most couldn't have put together such a resume; they were left behind wondering what they had done in the past twenty years that might stand out and look good on their resumes. More often than not, they were swept up in a tide of progress about which they'd fight and complain. They would find ways to jockey and position themselves on the periphery, their pride swelling, but the waves of merger would come crashing, scattering their thoughts and sending them to scramble and to put their humpty-dumpty together again.

In the break room, while refilling my coffee mug, I saw Minnow, our custodian. Everyone pronounced it Minner, and I had asked her a few years back how she came to have that name. She'd said, "My mama said my grandparents said when I was born, I was so little and shiny, I looked like a minnow. I guess they just kept on using it and I never thought nothing about it. Some kids called me fish bait in school, but I didn't pay them no mind and they quit." I'd chuckled and knew she probably made the smallest salary at the plant, so much so that we'd taken up a collection every year at Christmas. She raised her children by herself and then her grandchildren, too. Most had finished high school and gone to college with her help.

"You'll be alright, Minnow. You have always done an excellent job and they will keep you because none of them will do the work you do."

"I hope so. I'm gonna work until I fall over dead."

We both laughed and I refilled my mug.

It was sad to me, though, and I figured it would be to all the retired folks who had given their best years to the plant. While the merged plant would not erase history completely (not because they cared, but because they wanted to make sure and honor their own legacy and to use it for public relations purposes), there would be a new iteration unfolding, all in the name of efficiency and cost-savings. The hidden agenda, of course, was to inadvertently raise prices and to pay the consulting firm who put the merger together and who were cousins to a board member. Yes, progress, and this was the real trickle-down-economics people hear about from Washington.

The saddest will be the job loss. Employees would find other jobs at local insurance agencies, social services organizations, or in retail, but benefits would not be on par with what they'd had, if they got them at all. They would ultimately find that when they needed those benefits the most, they would no longer exist, and most employees knew it and were scared. My administrative assistant Kiwanis (named by her mother who took the name from the club sign on the "Welcome to the City" marquis she noticed on her way to give birth at the hospital) told me, "Without that insurance, I don't know what I'm gonna do when mine get sick, but I'll find that deadbeat ex-husband and make him pay his share. He's had it easy long enough." If the merger motivated others like Kiwanis, then it wouldn't be an all bad thing, and after all, history proves that time erases much.

Maxine

I've never met a librarian I didn't think was crazy. Sure, I admire them for reading books, for keeping knowledge organized and safe, for loaning books to everyone, for buying books and doing their part to keep the book business alive a while longer. I seem to gravitate to them and maybe that's because I come from a long line of librarians and crazy people myself, and maybe I teeter-totter on that line between what's normal and what's not, but Maxine went beyond eccentric to the far end of the deviancy spectrum.

I couldn't prove she killed her husbands, but something wasn't right. Her first husband had beat her, kept her and her children hidden away from society, and after several years she got the courage to escape through the woods when he was at work, making their way to a highway, where a trucker gave them a ride to the nearest town. They moved around and she finally divorced him through the mail, using a PO Box fifty miles from where she lived as her address, so he wouldn't come and stalk them. I admired Maxine for escaping abuse, going on to a community college, getting a head start on her education, jumping through all the hoops, and finally getting a bachelor's and then a master's in Library Science.

Her second husband died from a multitude of symptoms, no diagnosable illness, and the administrative assistant Hilda didn't think much about Maxine ordering books on poison until after the husband had been planted; no autopsy had been done either, because of religious reasons, though they had not attended church in the years they were married. Maxine met her next husband through an online Christian dating service, and after two years, he, too, passed under the same sort of strange circumstances and there were never any investigations. The thirty-year gap from the first husband she told people about and the death of her two husbands since she'd been at our library made us all wonder if there had been other husbands in between who had died.

Pushing sixty, Maxine didn't look like a killer. She was frumpy; much of her weight settled in the abdomen area, as if she were bloated from downing sodas for years, not drinking enough water. She came to work with us at the local Methodist College, having retired from one librarian job, looking for a second retirement because of our five year vesting option. Two retirements coupled with Social Security she believed would keep her going until her own demise. Her children, all grown and gone, didn't visit her much and she rescued cats and they scurried from window to window in her mid-town Cotswold-type cottage. Maxine had a small Prius that was paid for, but she walked the half-mile and back every day, bringing her sack lunch, to save money, she said.

The day Maxine came to the library with cuts all over her hands and arms was a game changer for most of us. When Hilda asked her, "What in the world happened to your hands and arms and have you been to the doctor?" Maxine said: "Two of my cats have leukemia and the vet wanted over two hundred dollars to put them to sleep. So, I decided to put them down myself and so one at a time, I held them under water in the bath tub until they were gone. They put up a fight, so they must not have been too sick. Next time, I guess I'll need to get me some of those industrial gloves."

O Christmas Tree

Nothing brings on the Christmas spirit more than going out to one of the local tree farms to choose and cut a live Christmas tree. We wanted to get one we could later plant, but those weren't available. Shopping for the tree, though, temporarily took our minds off of who wanted what from Santa and put us in an ethereal realm filled with pine scent, the same scent that attracted the likes of Rockefellers, Roosevelts, and Vanderbilts to the South. We drove the two-lane sand roads of the Christmas tree farm, tires smushing, scouting for the perfect tree and had a tough time making a decision: that one looked a little lopsided, that one had some dead limbs, that one seemed to have a bald spot. We searched for the model, the Marilyn Monroe of pines, which would look good with the glittery garland and blinking lights.

We drove deeper into the forest of Christmas trees past the Leyland Cypress, the Virginia Pine, and Eastern Red Cedar fields. We came full circle back to the wooden Christmas tree shed at the entrance with fresh Fraser Fir trees, hanging from fishing line on hooks on 2 x 4s jutting out of the eaves of the shed. Cut and shipped from the Appalachian mountains of North Carolina, the Frazier Christmas trees had just arrived. Their needles were soft to the touch and when shaken, the needles didn't fall to the ground like older trees that are water starved and spray painted to look fresh.

"How ya'll?" the old woman asked, grinning and showing spaces teeth used to occupy.

"Fine," I said, nodding. "You?"

"Can't complain." She wiped sweat beads from her forehead and shooed gnats. Even in early December, the temperatures were mild. She was heavy, with more weight in her feet and ankles than needed, and she heaved herself forward and up with a grunt.

"We got the nine feet over there, the eights here, the six and sevens mixed in over yonder. What ya'll want?"

"Seven."

She rocked back and forth to show me. The first one seemed fine. My wife and kids agreed. "We'll take it."

"Let me get somebody to wrap it, tie it to your roof." She rocked away.

A Mexican teenager, who would not make eye contact, appeared and cut the line, loaded it in a machine that shot it out wrapped in netting, and tied it to the roof rack of our 4-Runner. After I paid her, we took off, and sang along with a Christmas CD.

When we reached our house, I pressed the button on the garage opener, and once it was fully open, I drove in, catching limbs on the garage door and tearing the tree in several places. The perfect tree looked like a cleared strip on a mountain side where electrical lines ran. Sadly, I had actually forgotten about the perfect Christmas tree being on the roof and didn't think it was so high it would have caught on the garage door. My kids screamed and cried, and my wife was telling me she could not believe I'd done that after I'd paid fifty dollars for the tree.

"It'll be alright. I'll trim it right. You'll see," I said. I didn't think it would be alright and I felt heat in my chest and tingling in my feet, the same way I'd felt when I couldn't hold it any longer as a child and finally had felt the warmth running down my leg and puddling at my feet.

I untied the tree from the roof rack, pulled it off, screwed the tree to the red and green plastic stand, and trimmed with pruning shears. I moved it to the dining room, and while it looked less like Marilyn Monroe and more like Don Knotts, I turned the shredded side to the wall, humming "O Christmas tree." My wife didn't think it was funny, but agreed, with a smirk, it looked "okay." The children didn't notice, and when Santa came, he found a place for gifts. I wondered about the stout lady at the Christmas tree farm and the Hispanic teen who would not look at me and wondered if they'd had a good holiday. I suspected they might be closer to the meaning of the holiday than we were.

First Pitch

I tried to like baseball when I was a kid, but I didn't. I couldn't throw or catch, but I could run. Because of imagination, I don't often pay much attention to anyone or anything, hence not a star pupil as old yellowed and musty report cards clearly reflect. A friend of mine's dad even took me and him to Atlanta to see the Braves' Hank Aaron play, but I was more interested in the planes coming and going and the Atlanta skyline from the Braves stadium than the game.

This backdrop made for an interesting reaction when I was asked to throw out the first pitch at the University of Memphis and Middle Tennessee State University baseball game held at the Jackson Generals (B team for Seattle Mariners) stadium in Jackson, Tennessee. At first, I was flabbergasted. I couldn't actually recall when I'd thrown a baseball. It had to be elementary school or when I was involved with the Royal Ambassadors at the Baptist church, where I'd used the Lord's name in vain when I got hit by a baseball and nearly got thrown out of the church. The minister had come to visit with my parents; they'd been exasperated with me, but knew that no amount of churching was going to stop the invasion of genes I'd inherited from wilder relatives on both their sides.

In addition to my initial reaction, I wondered why they'd chosen me until one of the athletic department public relations officials said, "You've got to be pretty good if you're related to Josh." Josh Reddick from the Oakland A's, formerly from the Boston Red Sox. Yes, I had been asked by people from time to time, and what I said was, "Yes, we are distant cousins, and I've never met him." No matter how bad I wanted to name-drop and make connections, a true Southern behavior, I never misrepresented. So, I laughed that off and told my wife and kids three days before the big event I needed to practice.

We went into the front yard. I marked off sixty feet and six inches from the edge of the driveway and my son Nicholas and daughter Audrey got their gloves and I started moving my arm up and down and around to make sure it wouldn't come out of its socket. I must have looked like an idiot to anyone driving by our house.

After a few minutes, though, I had to admit I wasn't bad at all. Out of forty something throws each night before the big game, almost every one of my throws had been sixty feet and six inches and dead center. One did go into the road, and one did hit the bricks on the house, but the others were excellent. I felt good and confident and though my shoulder had a numbing pain from activating long dormant muscles and ligaments that probably had shriveled and disconnected from lack of use through the years, I felt okay, like maybe I wouldn't end up in the emergency room or kill someone as I had almost done golfing years before when my ball knocked someone's dad unconscious at the driving range.

On the night of the first pitch, the weather wasn't good. It was projected to rain. I had bought a long sleeve shirt, school colors, to wear and I asked my kids to accompany me because there were TV cameras and I thought when I'm dead and gone, it would be a good memory for them. They introduced me over the loudspeaker and television cameras were recording as I stepped up to the mound, beautifully raked reddish brown soil, base plates clean and white, and grass manicured and green. It was a stark contrast to the last days of winter, as if spring was just around the corner. I think I was so nervous that I didn't pay attention at all and just threw the ball, sixty feet and six inches, square onto home plate. "Great pitch," the catcher said, when my ball hit his glove and some of the crowd clapped.

I had done it. I had proven I could and then I had fantasies that maybe I was really better than I remembered all those years ago, and on the way home, I told my kids I should have played baseball more.

Heart Attack

We were in the vehicle on the interstate traveling to see my dad for his birthday and to have a family dinner when my sister called to say she thought he was having a heart attack and was taking him to the hospital. Other than a handful of colds through his seventy plus years and one case of food poisoning, my dad had been the ultimate mind-over-matter-vitamin and herb-man. I often wondered if he really had the mind-over-matter power, if he could will his heart to heal.

Though dad never said it, I know he must have thought me and my two brothers and sister were wimps for our bouts with mumps, chicken pox, flu, and the worst of all, allergies. We often took stuff we didn't know we were taking to avoid a doctor's bill, and to this day, we all believe in a concoction for chest colds called Numol, a mixture of natural oils that had a medicinal smell that was once made in Atlanta and has since long faded from the market. The last place we could get it was Pic-N-Save, a chain drug and department store that finally closed when all the new on-every-corner-drug- stores appeared. It seemed ten times as strong as Vicks' VapoRub.

Three years ago, my dad and I had about a quarter inch left between us and I mentioned to a family friend who worked at a local family-owned pharmacy that I felt a cold coming on and would probably use the last of the Numol I'd been saving for years. She was astounded I knew what Numol was and said she could compound some for me. I was elated and knew I would have enough bottles made to give every one of my family members one for Christmas. They weren't quite as excited about it as I had been, especially as a Christmas gift.

We were about twenty-five miles away and I heard my wife on her cell: "Yes, oh no. You're going to the hospital? Is he okay? Did the ambulance come?" My own heart was pounding. I looked at her and she mouthed "Your dad." I know tears welled in my eyes, but I tried to hide it, and I turned on the hazard lights and increased speed. She convinced me I didn't need to speed or have the hazard lights on, that he was fully conscious, just in pain. When we exited the interstate, I couldn't go to the hospital. I wasn't ready. I don't avoid confrontation. I simply wasn't ready to deal with the fact that my dad might be dying, so we stopped by a store to pick up some items we needed. When we got to the hospital, my dad lay in a hospital bed with monitors and an IV. He was jovial, said he felt fine and thought he'd be leaving shortly. I later learned that what they give those who are suffering heart attacks actually opens the blood vessels and alleviates pain. Mom smiled and shook her head indicating he wasn't leaving. My sister told me in the waiting room that preliminary tests indicated he was in the process of having a massive heart attack and they wanted to run further tests to which he would not consent, maintaining it was under control. My mother signed the papers for the hospital and he was angry with her.

Upstairs on the cardiac unit, he underwent additional tests, all of which took longer than we were told, so we naturally worried. The doctor called us in and told us he'd had a massive heart attack, there was damage, and there was considerable blockage. He needed bypass surgery the next day. Dad told the doctor he had something at home that might take care of the blockage, and the doctor smiled and told him that the only thing that was going to keep him alive was having the surgery. Dad said he'd think about it.

My wife and kids left to go home, and I stayed with my mom and sister in the waiting room until visiting hours were over. Mom seemed frailer than I had noticed, and her hands shook. She had a special cushion she carried around that helped with the back pain she experienced on a daily basis, pain left over from botched surgery. I drove her home, and we got up early, drank coffee, and went back to the hospital to learn if there were new developments. My sister met us there, and I figured she would have made a great investigative reporter. She had called folks all over town to see who'd had heart surgery, who had performed the surgery, who was good and who was not. She learned one doctor was known to drink and one had a bad track record. She learned two were top-notch, and by the time we arrived, she already learned that at least one of them was available for dad's surgery.

Mom visited first and took about twenty minutes. When she came out, she was crying and mumbled he'd agreed to the surgery. My sister and I visited with him next. She tried to be strong, to keep her sense of humor, but she couldn't do it. I told him all would go well, that his other sons were coming and would be here when he awoke. Quite frankly, I didn't know if he'd wake or not. One of the nurses, a friend I'd known in high school reassured me, telling me he was an excellent candidate, which sounded like he was applying for a job. They wheeled his bed out of the room and down a different corridor, and I'm sure he was nervous and scared. I'd had surgery twice myself (not as serious as dad's), and each time I was a nervous wreck. On the second surgery, I begged them to knock me out simply because I kept thinking the worst and thought I'd have a heart attack.

Once we were in the waiting room, there wasn't much to do. I began working on my laptop as did my sister. One of our brothers showed and visited with others in the waiting room, including a distantly related family from mom's side. An hour or so into the surgery, several people from dad's church and family friends showed up to keep us company. We had to recount the story---how dad was actually at the funeral home working when he had his heart attack (a job he'd taken after he retired from the automobile dealership because he got to visit people and socialize). He was too sick to drive the hearse and so rather than go to the hospital, a half-block from the funeral home (which would be the window view for any patient on the right side of the hospital), he decided to go home and try and rest, hoping the nausea, the pain, the numbness would all come to an end. When he finally decided to let my sister drive him, he waited for another thirty minutes on my mom to "fix" her hair, put on some make-up, and get dressed. All agreed it was a miracle he wasn't dead. I noted to myself had he gone earlier he might not have to have the by-pass surgery.

The waiting room was cramped and I looked at my mom who was clearly not as nervous and my sister said she'd taken several valium. In fact, she didn't look much there at all. I wondered if she was hallucinating as she was focused on a Monet on the wall, a late impressionistic piece from his garden at Giverny. I recalled a similar painting I focused on when I had my wisdom teeth removed over twenty-five years ago, and I still remembered after being medicated the sensation of flowing into the wheat field on the wall where I ran and laughed and played until they shook me awake after the surgery, a mouth full of gauze, lips and cheeks swollen and bruised, but light as balloons like the lyrics from a Pink Floyd song.

The phone rang and one of our distant relatives answered it. He called for my mother, "It's for you," and she asked who it was. When he told her it was her mother, I half-smiled and laughed and looked at my sister who was doing the same. Mom, in her drug induced state, gripped the chair rails to help pull herself up to take the call. My sister shook her head, but I couldn't pass up the opportunity. "Mom," I said, and she turned toward me and said, "Yes?" "Don't answer it," I said, laughing. She looked at me as if I was crazy and kept moving. "No, honey, you must have the wrong number," she told the woman on the other end of the line. Then, she shuffled back to her chair. My brother even looked over at us as if he didn't understand why my mom would answer a phone call from her mother, who had been deceased for over five years.

Shortly after, one of the assistants to the surgeon came out and told us all was going well, but they had to do six by-passes instead of four and it would take longer than anticipated. We were all shocked, and I could tell by the looks on others' faces that they hadn't heard of anyone having six by-passes before. In fact, one of my dad's friends had undergone by-pass surgery and offered us an account, which, of course, none of us wanted to hear.

At some point, the surgeon came out and told us all went well. They didn't have any trouble restarting his heart. The fact that they had actually stopped his heart had somehow eluded me earlier. They told us not to be afraid when we go in to visit, that he would look rather traumatized with a taped tube in his throat, more monitors, and IVs. He didn't seem that bad off when I glanced in on him after a while. I was just relieved---relieved he was still tough and could survive it all, relieved that he would be around a little longer. I was even more relieved that night when they took the tube out, he was awake and sitting up in his bed. He stayed for about a week at the hospital before going home, and it took a few weeks for him to get back to his normal routine of helping bury those who didn't make it.

A Porsche for Me

For my Dad and Grandmother

When I turned sixteen, I hoped for a car. As morning faded into afternoon, and my grandparents, aunts, uncles and cousins drifted in for a free meal and cake, I came to realize I was not getting a car. What made me think I would I don't know. Just because my dad ran service and parts areas for an automobile dealership didn't mean we had money. The lack of air conditioning in our rented hundred-year-old clapboard house with a rusted tin roof, attic fan sucking in dust, exhaust from tractor trailers on highway 41, and the occasional skunk spray were all proof of poverty. Even more, my siblings and I got one pair of tennis shoes from Sears at the beginning of the school year that was to last us a year, and hand-me-downs from our older cousins came in recycled grocery store paper bags when we visited my grandmother on Sunday afternoons after church.

Visiting her was proof it wasn't just us who were poor. It was the generation before, too. We sat on the porch swing, sweat beads trickling down our backs, in the South Georgia heat, and fanned with funeral home fans trying to stay awake while my grandmother talked about relatives, ailments, and church to my dad as they all rocked in rocking chairs with paint flaking. Passers-by could see the family huddled on the porch, surrounded by hanging baskets, pots full of all sorts of plants, some of which were used for cures and others that added beauty to my grandmother's sinking and leaning house. From one end to the other, the house had shifted and made me feel like I was going into the ground or coming out of the ground, depending on my direction.

"What you need a car for?" my Grandmother asked.

"Go places."

"Ain't nowhere to go around here," she said.

"Maybe go on a date."

"Leave the girls alone. Time for that later. Them girls just want to trap you. Get you a job, start saving up for some dirt."

"Dirt?"

"Yep. Once you get you some land, you can get a house, plant a garden."

"Yes ma'am."

It didn't do any good to argue with her and while we all loved her, she hadn't been anywhere, didn't know the potential a car would bring. She'd never learned to drive, mainly relying on others for rides to the grocery store or church. Sometimes, she'd walk, but as she'd aged, she relied on others more. A broad and stout woman, she would have been a linebacker and played football had she been a man. She cooked better than anyone in the family. First time my mother met her, my grandmother made my mother make biscuits to prove she could cook for my dad.

At some point dad would interject, "Well, we best be getting on home." My grandmother would try to get us to stay. Baths, school the next day, homework all became my mom's reassurance we needed to get home. Besides, we hated staying there. The walls weren't painted and we imagined eyes of monsters in the wood.

Our skin stuck to the vinyl seats of my mom's 1966 Buick Skylark as we drove the twenty minutes home, windows down and bugs zinging our skin in the backseat. When we got home, I noticed for the first time how empty our backyard seemed without a car for me parked there. The football, last tag, hide and seek we'd played through the years no longer had meaning. Had it not been for my dad's job, he wouldn't have a car at all. He got to drive a car from the lot every day—sometimes it might be a customer's car that he needed to hear and feel to better understand the complaint and sometimes it might be a brand new car. We were the envy of our friends when dad drove unique vehicles home and we rode around in town: The Thing, a convertible Bug, or the Rabbit. We didn't feel poor because of that and because we always had food to eat.

A week later, I had driven mom's car to town to shop for records at K-Mart, and stopped at the shop to visit my dad. He was standing at the wooden blue desk where he stood doing paperwork on cars for forty-five years. I noticed a baby blue Mustang II on the lot and mentioned it to my dad. He said, "Come out back. I got something to show you." We walked out back to the fenced in jungle of wrecked cars, junk cars that were used for parts. It had been a treasure hunting ground for me when I was younger, finding money in ashtrays, ball bearings used for marbles, or an occasional toy left behind.

"You see that?" he asked.

"Yeah, I see that junk car," I said sarcastically.

"You can have it. We'll get you some tires, a new engine, paint it. Be good as new. I can get it fixed for next to nothing."

"What is it?" I walked around it feeling sick to my stomach.

"A Porsche."

"I don't want a junk car. I'd rather buy that Mustang."

"How you gonna pay for that?""I got a job bussing tables at the motel restaurant by the interstate."

"Okay, then, go talk to one of the salesman."

I did talk to the salesman, and for the next two and a half years, I had a car payment that took almost two weeks of pay per month. The Mustang II was used with 35k miles, formerly owned by a young preacher. The air conditioning didn't cool and needed repair; it cost too much and since I didn't have the money, I rolled down the windows or turned the glass vents in to get a breeze. I didn't care. It was mine and looked better than my mom's car. The next weekend, I drove separately to my grandmother's and took her for a spin.

"This is nice," she said.

"Want to drive?"

"No, I ain't got any use driving a car and you be careful. That light's gonna change, so slow down. Let those people behind you know you're gonna stop by tapping your breaks." For someone who didn't drive, she did well offering instruction.

Five years later, three front-end wrecks that landed several people in the hospital, and a hundred and thirty-five thousand miles, I sold the Mustang II. I bought a silver Buick Regal with velvet seats and electric windows. I felt uptown. While I have long regretted not taking the complimentary Porsche, I have come to rationalize that because of my wrecks, I would not have lived had I taken the Porsche because the front end was hollow, the engine in the back.

History

Jason Lanier had served in public relations at Altamaha College for twenty-five years. A lean, distinguished fellow with thinning hair and a slight comb-over, Jason had once worked on local television until the first president he had worked for at Altamaha lured him away with a little more salary and better benefits. Raises, though, had not been regular in the state of Georgia and benefits tanked despite tax hikes through the years to solve financial woes. If Jason could do the math, he would learn he'd actually lost more money through the years than he would have if he'd stayed on at the local TV station making the same salary.

Jason's most recent, and sixth, president he worked for was a politician. It was a miracle that Jason had survived twenty-five years, with all of the presidents being different. President Madison Lester had been able to secure funding for the neglected college, but his attitude toward employees had sent morale to an all-time low. There were many times he didn't acknowledge employees at all, passing them in the halls, and he didn't attend many events at the college because of fictitious appointments when he had been sighted at a local pub with other politicians. He also bullied employees, and when ideas where raised he considered shallow, he played the role of gadfly, like Socrates.

Jason had seen the path to president change from an academic one to one of business leaders, lawyers, and politicians being selected by systems to run colleges and universities, and the college machines ran better and were more efficient. Standards had dropped, enrollment had increased, and funding had increased.

Jason tapped on the door frame of President Lester's office and Lester was busy typing an email on his computer. "Yeah."

"You want to work on the story?"

"Come on in. Let me finish this."

Jason sat in the wing back chair, looking around the office at the photos of handshakes of Lester with politicians and donors, one black and white of Lester and his wife some twenty years prior at a ball, and a black and white photo of Lester's parents by a convertible in Florida with a beach backdrop. Jason wondered if desk and office photos were extensions of personas, how they attempt to fool others, how lying always comes back to haunt, and why he had to have a role in this. He knew he couldn't retire, needed the money with one child in college, a wife struggling with depression and diabetes, his house not paid off, insurance bills mounting. He hated playing along, no more than he liked playing kickball at recess when older, bigger students always won or playing hit the piñata with adults guiding the blindfolded guests so they didn't hit the piñata and get all the candy and saved it for the birthday boy. Jason knew he had to play along and wondered how Lester might want to spin Ansley's departure.

"Alright. What you got?"

"Well, I was thinking we could start the article with Ansley's previous work and accomplishments, then the donations that came while she was here, the growth we saw in the pre- law program, and then how she's moving on to better things and how we're better for her having been here."

Jason didn't know what Lester wanted exactly, but knew he didn't want the truth in the newspaper---that Ansley and Lester had been spotted doggie style in the dark room by the photography faculty member late in the afternoon when faculty were normally gone and had told a few folks. Unfortunately, he was up for tenure with a MFA, and the President already determined the faculty member would be gone, despite recommendations from a department head and dean, who also served at the pleasure of the president; the rumor had eventually made its way to the Baptist church, and even Ms. Lester had gotten wind of it. Rumor was Ms. Lester threatened to put him on the road if he didn't put Ansley on the road first. Of course, the president had denied the sex act, had denied earlier rumors of taking a bribe in the form of a special allocation for a building project to hire her from a congressman in Atlanta, had denied he'd broken human resources policy in hiring her, had denied that her pre-law program stole students from the Humanities because of her broken promises to students of law school admissions, had denied private money was being funneled to the foundation from her family to provide study abroad experiences to pre law students and paying her huge stipends.

Lester reared back in his chair, three his oxblood wingtips on the desk. "Include she was popular among the students."

"Okay."

"Mention that as founder of the pre-law program, she recruited more students than any other program on campus."

"Right." Jason knew that she technically had, but those students didn't come from outside the institution; they were baling on other majors.

"Make sure to include that donations to that department were at an all-time high under her leadership."

"Okay." Jason knew that was also technically true, but there was no leadership and donations came from family to the foundation only to come back out of the foundation to her.

"She resurrected study abroad for the institution, something that hadn't happened in years."

"Yes sir."

"Jason, you know, these deadbeat academics just don't get it. They're clueless. They need to get off their lazy asses and do stuff."

"Touché." Jason laughed, stroking Lester's ego, and regretting he'd said it. "I'll shoot you a draft today."

Jason left the president's office, exchanged pleasantries with Paula, his administrative assistant, but felt drained and tired and sick to his stomach. He knew he could rationalize most of the article and would try and stick to the facts, not adding in too many positive adjectives. That would make Jason feel better about writing what would become history. He knew Lester would throw him under the bus to anyone who questioned the article—at home, on campus, or in the community. He'd done it before: "That's not what I told him to write," or "You can't tell anybody to do anything anymore" or "I'm supposed to review it and it went out without my approval." Jason knew when the article was published, most wouldn't read it because readership had declined through the years at the newspaper. Those who did read it wouldn't wonder why there were no stories for other employees who'd left the college. Jason just hoped he could make another year since staying one more would increase his bring home when combined with Social Security upon retirement.

When he reached the top of the stairs, which he always took to try and strengthen his calves, his loafer caught on a lose nail and he lunged forward, tumbling down the stairs and landing catawampus and unconscious. Jason regained consciousness some time the next week in the hospital with casts on an arm and leg and didn't recall anything about that day he fell---the meeting, the article, the fall. The administrative assistant had taken over temporarily and written the article for the paper. During rehabilitation, the Human Resources manager visited Jason and explained how he could be on temporary disability for six months, and then use his annual and sick leave putting him on target to retire with even more income. Jason took the deal, and the administrative assistant wrote a piece for the paper on Jason's long career.

Damascus Road

When I backed into the parked car I didn't see in a well-lit parking garage, I thought I might have had a seizure or something. A few days later, my daughter was riding with me after a high school soccer game and I said, "You see that deer over there? If it starts moving toward the road, let me know."

"What deer?"

"Good night! Can't you see it?" I pointed.

"Dad, that's not a deer. It's a hedge."

"Oh," I said. I still slowed the vehicle.

A week later, I finally decided to get a follow-up and see if my vision had deteriorated. After the hour wait, I read the eye chart as best I could. I couldn't see the bottom two lines at all and told the assistant: "I don't believe anyone could see that. Besides, the only thing that small would be bugs and if you could see the detail of them splattering on the windshield, it would make you sick." The doctor's assistant smirked. When the doctor finally made it in, I asked him if my eyesight was worse. "No," he said, "It's as bad as it was last year and the year before that when we checked it. You really ought to have those cataracts removed. I don't know how you are even driving."

"Well, will insurance cover it?"

"Yes."

"Do you do the surgery?"

"No, we refer to the Surgery Center."

"Is it safe?"

"Yes, it should be. It only takes about ten minutes and they'll give you something that will relax you completely."

"Alright. I'm in."

"Good, we'll set it up for Monday around lunch. The nurses will give you some instructions."

"Thanks," I said, and he nodded, grabbed my chart, and went out the door.

The next Monday seemed to pass slowly. I had strict directions that I could not eat or drink after midnight and I felt starved. My stomach rumbled and I was anxious. I didn't have to wait long before a nurse called out my name and I followed her into the unit. I removed my shoes and climbed on the bed. They didn't make me disrobe. Directions to remove any dentures or jewelry followed by questions about drug allergies and confirmation I hadn't had food or drink came before an IV, blood pressure cuff, and heart rate monitor. One of the nurses brought me a pill and said, "Swallow this. It will help you relax. It's Xanax. Your blood pressure is a little high."

A few minutes later, another nurse came in, told me this would also help me rest, and shot Versed into the IV. When I woke in the same bed, with a warm blanket on top of me, the nurse said, "How do you feel?"

"Fine," said. I had a patch over my eye and she asked, "What would you like to drink?"

"Diet coke with ice."

"Okay, would you prefer crackers or cookies?"

"Cookies," I said. "What kind of cookies?"

"Fudge striped."

"Yes. I haven't had those in a while."

I got home, ate lunch, and went to bed. I slept for three hours, woke up, and watched all the bad news with my remaining bad eye. The next morning, I enjoyed coffee before my follow-up. The nurse removed the bandage, cleaned the gunk around the eye, and told me to read the charts. Not only could I read the chart again, the letters were bold and clear. It was amazing. As I left the office with instructions to put three different types of drops in my eye, I was stunned at color, the detail. I could see cracks in the asphalt in the parking lot, details of clouds, leaves and pine needles on trees. I saw dust particles in the air. When I got home, I went to a mirror and noted aside from the bloodshot and swollen eye, I could see where I'd missed hairs in a shave, noted an ear hair and nose hair I hadn't seen earlier. Everything was so clear that it was almost overwhelming at times and I felt wobbly. It was as if I had been like the biblical character Paul on the Damascus Road, blinded by the light, or if *Amazing Graze* should be my theme song with its verse: "I was blind, but now I see." I was appreciative and felt I'd been given a second chance to see the world. I wanted to shout the message of cataract surgery from the mountain tops and in the days that followed I began to evangelize to cashiers at the grocery store, waiters in restaurants, and employees at work.

After a week, I had the second eye surgery. It went as well as the first and I was no less impressed. About a week later, after the swelling and redness were gone, and my vision was 20/20, I came home to bills from the surgeon, surgery center, anesthetist, and my optometrist, No one bothered to tell me my insurance did not *fully* cover the surgery because it was considered "elective". While I knew they couldn't repossess my new lens implants, I chose to pay them anyway.

The Graduate Cabin

After I earned a Philosophy degree, I didn't know what to do, and as a first generation college graduate, I often heard echoes from family who hadn't gone to college: "What the hell is Philosophy?" or "What the hell can you do with that?" or "Sounds like a waste of time and money to me!" I hadn't really thought about employment. Besides, I had a job working as a desk clerk in a hotel. When I thought about things I might enjoy, I had several ideas and applied for a variety of jobs: driving the Marta monorail in Atlanta, teaching in a private school out West for Native Americans, working for the federal government in an embassy overseas, to name a few. I spent a lot of time before the internet in the library searching for places to send my resume, spent a lot of time typing letters, and spent a lot of money at the post office sending my resume first class in nice cardboard envelopes to keep the resume from tearing or getting wrinkled. No one ever called. One of my professors suggested that if I couldn't find a job, maybe I should go to Graduate school.

I had recently become interested in parapsychology after having some strange experiences during the night when I worked at a local Air Force base. I'd seen a UFO one night on my way to the base. It was round and lights were flashing. My camera wasn't in my car, but I did pull over, stood outside, and hoped it might abduct me. Unfortunately, it took off quickly and with no sound, and I drove on to work. There hadn't been any sort of lapse in time, so I couldn't claim abduction. Military folks I knew said it wasn't ours, but they told me confidentially we had some. I would assume they used them to spy or for some undercover operations.

I was fascinated with stories of ghosts ever since I'd seen one in our old house when I was a teenager, and I was interested in dreams and their potential meaning. I also believed I was intuitive and gifted, though I flunked the gifted exams in elementary school. I had a tough time having imaginary friends, too, telling my playmates it seemed like a dumb concept. My mother reinforced my interest in the paranormal: "Yes, I always thought you were different even as a baby in your crib when drawers from your chest-of-drawers were pulled out in your bedroom when I'd come in." I was the oldest and only child for my first two years, so it couldn't have been done by a sibling, but they could have easily been left open by my young stressed mother. I also believed in Bigfoot from personal experience. I had been home alone in our farm house one evening, and the wood-knock on the house brought me outside with a flashlight. I then saw something by the barn with red eyes that was about nine feet tall and covered in hair, and I jumped in my car and drove over to some friends' house to spend the night. There had been screams and other sightings in our rural area along the tea-colored water of the Little River; the stories even made the newspaper and TV.

I finally made up my mind to go to a very unique Psychology Graduate program that offered courses in parapsychology in the mountains of Northern Georgia, and I rented a room in the Graduate cabin. I looked for the sign to the red clay-rock road named Jay Bird lane, which led to the Graduate cabin. I hadn't met my four roommates, but they had all been accepted or were already enrolled in Graduate school and had rented rooms from Dr. Robert Thomas, a retired professor who'd built onto the original log structure with rock floors and rented rooms to supplement state retirement pay. He and his wife, who we never saw, lived a short distance from the Graduate cabin on Jay Bird. Dr. Thomas reassured there were no bears or snakes on this side of the mountain. He wore Jesus sandals, his toes curled, and his toenails were thick. His knees angled in when he walked, and while he talked, he smoothed wisps of hair.

I didn't feel comfortable looking into the rooms of my cabin mates, but I looked around the kitchen, the back porch, and the great room. My room had a great view of the deep gulch below. The furnishings were sparse and looked like rejects from Goodwill. The Styrofoam in the sofa cushions poked through rips like fat rolls squeezing out of tight clothes, and the whole house smelled musty and damp. I learned my first night darkness came early in the woods and seemed colder, particularly when there was rain and fog.

I made some chicory coffee, sipped it, and smoked cigarettes on the porch until dusk. I came in and closed the door that didn't lock, a perfect target for a mountain man ax murderer. I felt better that my bedroom door locked, and I even put a straight chair under the knob for added security. I had a radio to tune out any screams from a Bigfoot roaming the woods. My NPR classic station combined with a ceiling fan on high kept me sleeping through the night and I woke early to a seemingly empty house. I took a quick shower and made coffee downstairs. I noted a car in the yard from the kitchen window. I had no idea which roommate it was until about lunch when a woman with frizzed red hair wearing a long nightgown and terry cloth robe with Barbie bedroom slippers shuffled into the kitchen. She came from the only downstairs bedroom on the back of the house.

"Got coffee?"

"Yes."

"You Kyle?"

"Yes. You?"

"Call me Roz. This is my second year. I work as a counselor in the afternoon and evening at the youth hospital here. I do art therapy."

"Cool," I said. "Where're you from? Obviously not the South."

"Right. I'm from Massachusetts. I'm a witch."

"Oh, I don't think so. You seem extremely nice."

"No, I'm Wiccan."

"What's that?"

"I practice Wicca. Witchcraft. Want a Tarot card reading?"

"Sure. What's a Tarot card reading?" I was still trying to recover from the witch comments and visualized a young Endora character from *Bewitched*. I also wondered what the rest of these Graduate students were going to be like and if I'd made a mistake renting a room at the Graduate cabin."Where are you from, Kyle?"

"Small, farming town in middle Tennessee."

"Ah, a Southern boy. I do declare," she said in a fake Southern accent, flipping her hair. "I'll get the cards. You'll love it." As she moved toward her bedroom, she yelled back over her shoulder, "Oh, and I'm a lesbian now, so don't get any ideas."

"Okay," I said. I had never known a lesbian either. I hadn't even started the program and I had already experienced at least three new things.

When Roz returned, she shuffled the cards and placed three face down. When she turned them face up, they were the Queen of Cups, Queen of Wands, and Five of Coins.

"Oh, this is special, Kyle. The Queen of Cups has never turned up in a reading I've done. This is a powerful, caring, and nurturing sign. The Queen of Wands is also a powerful sign—fertile, feminine, and representing positive energy. The Five of Coins is a less positive card, but it can mean financial strain, insecurity, and trepidation. In your new situation, you probably feel these things, but your overall spirit of power is going to carry you through. This is an excellent sign for you, Kyle"

"Great. I think I'll be fine, too. I appreciate your doing a reading, Roz." I didn't want to tell her, but it didn't seem much different than the horoscope in the newspaper--general and not specific at all. It seemed to me that people often needed to hear meaning when, in fact, they could find the meaning themselves without a Tarot reading or horoscope. I didn't think it was necessarily evil or that Roz was going to hell as I had heard preached while growing up in the rural Pentecostal church, but I also understood the caution of relying on others and gimmicks to find happiness or solve problems.

When the door opened and the fellow walked through in fatigues, with a rifle across one shoulder and an Army green duffle bag across his other shoulder, I thought about paying Dr. Thomas a visit to demand a lock, but Roz said, "Hey, Doug".

Doug responded, "Roz, how you been?"

"You been hunting?""No, just carry it for protection."

Roz went on to introduce us, and I noted Doug sounded a bit like Jack Nicholson and had a little crazy in his eyes, too. I learned Doug had been in the Army, had been stationed in the South Korean demilitarized zone for several years, and was taking advantage of the free educational benefits from the federal government. I offered to give him a hand and took his duffle up to his room, where he had an arsenal of knives, other guns, cans of food, and books all stacked neatly. Part of me was glad to have him in the Graduate cabin without a lock and especially next to my room. Prior to going into the Army and coming to the university, Doug had been a plumber in New York. I shook his hand and turned to go out, and he farted. I turned back and he said, "Sorry, the cabbage in kimchi gives me gas, but the shit is good. You eat it?"

"Never had it"

"I'll cook us some soon."

"Okay," I said. "Good to meet you, Doug." I headed back down to get my coffee and sit outside. Roz had apparently gone back to her room to cast spells or something. Later, another vehicle pulled into the yard. The couple who exited seemed like they had just come from a medieval movie set. Tristan was dressed in armor, a sword at his side, and a helmet under an arm while Elizabeth wore a long dress, tight in the abdomen and adorned with beads, with flowing see-through material from the shoulders. Both spoke in accents that reminded me of faraway lands in the British Isles. In reality, they both hailed from the Pocono region of Pennsylvania. The Graduate cabin seemed complete and contrary to society, the minority in society had become the majority at the cabin, and I felt like a minority for the first time in my life—a loner and odd man out. I already wondered if I would make it through a graduate program that I felt had far more flavor than my vanilla life.

As the seasons passed, classes and reading seemed to absorb most of my time. There were student activities such as mock therapy sessions, past life regression hypnosis sessions, barbecues by the river, and cookouts at an eccentric faculty member's house on July 4th when to celebrate freedom, he'd shoot fireworks at the university president's house across the street, but the one I enjoyed most was a concert with the Indigo Girls. At the concert in the gym, I sat on a bench by an exit and a middle aged lady who looked familiar walked in, said hello, and asked if I was enjoying the concert. I assured her I was and figured she might be a faculty member. We made small talk for a few minutes. Turned out, it was Joan Baez and she did a guest appearance with the Indigo Girls. It was a moment I never forgot and I listened to their cassettes until they broke several years later.

I was fascinated with my faculty members: former students of Carl Jung, Abraham Maslow, and other trail blazers; best-selling authors who were often on popular television shows such as *Unsolved Mysteries*; faculty who had investigated hauntings and odd occurrences such as the Amityville case, the ship Queen Mary, and possession cases; Buddhist, Consciousness, and Phenomenology experts; and even editors of international journals, where I served as an editorial assistant. The department was a smorgasbord of exotic courses I enjoyed sampling. It also attracted the fringes of society: students in search of leprechauns and fairies; students who believed they'd led previous lives of fame and acted out those roles in their current lives; and even students who believed they had psychic powers. In sum, many of them weren't much different than my childhood friends and their imaginary playmates; they had simply grown up and taken their imaginations to new levels.

Whether it was giggling downstairs from Roz' room, the clicking of guns from Doug's room (I had watched him from my window shoot a stray dog for sport and take him by the back legs and sling him into the gulch below), the scraping of swords in Tristan and Elizabeth's room, or my deviating even more from my Southern conservative upbringing, I often had trouble sleeping. Like Huck Finn, I enjoyed my freedom while in my own river of thought, but each time I had to deal with others in the Graduate Cabin, life seemed more stressful.

When a famous French psychic came to guest lecture, we formed a circle and she walked around "reading" each of us Graduate students. I wondered what I had gotten myself into. A tarot card reading for fun was one thing, but integrating psychic readings into a Graduate curriculum seemed a bit much. It wasn't that I didn't believe such was possible; it was that if there were some sort of magic, power, or secrets out there, then someone should have "fixed" the world with that knowledge. I wondered why people continued to display evil to each other, why people continued to suffer from disease and die, and why humanity didn't use new technology to advance more rather than control or profit.

With my 4.0 grade point average, I landed an assistantship and moved out of the Graduate cabin and into a garage apartment behind the dumpster at the A&P just down from the college's entrance. I realized that most of the Graduate students I had known were there for themselves. They were trying to find answers to life's puzzles they would not find, trying to heal from evil done to them, or trying to understand their own difference. Some wanted to help others. In order to help, though, there had to be a desire to be helped, and if that was absent, then help often couldn't be obtained. What I needed was to live alone, so I could focus on learning as much as I could with the least amount of distractions.

I never knew what happened to Tristan and Elizabeth, but I heard their romance had not lasted after they completed the program. Doug, unfortunately, blew his brains out in his second year. He got off several automatic rounds before he lost muscle control in his arm. The bullet spray went through the wall into my vacant room and I had to wonder if I would have been killed if I had stayed on at the Graduate cabin. His body was shipped to New York for burial, but I don't think anyone from our program could afford the trip to attend. When I got his home address, I sent his parents a card. Last I heard, Roz hiked South America with her giggling friend, worked with shamans, and had drug-induced visions.

After graduation, I began to work with the state in social services. It seemed to me as the years passed that the Graduate cabin and program were some of the best experiences of my life. The experiences taught me to be less judgmental and to appreciate and look past difference and to our shared humanity. I grew to appreciate and love my faculty who had really helped me to peer into doors I might have simply passed by in a hallway. Finally, all of the searching allowed me to come back home, to my own place in the world, and work to make it just a little better.

Staying Close

We're all crowded at the Sand Dollar condo on Crescent Beach, Florida, and I hope the condo inspection team doesn't come around. We had just enough beds to sleep eight adults, and we brought three air mattresses to sleep the six children. We weren't expecting my nephew to bring his girlfriend and we weren't expecting my niece to bring her friend. The upstairs toilet has been clogged twice, the air conditioning is running twenty-four hours and hasn't made it to seventy-four degrees, and my sister-in-law is eight months pregnant and snoring all night.

Even with the door closed, we can all hear her, but we don't say anything because we fear it could deform the baby or something, but this baby is doomed with his gene pool from the start. Mama already broke a plate, sweeping chards off the tile floor and saying, "They won't ever miss just one," and Dad has broken the rusted pull chains on two ceiling fans trying to turn them counter-clockwise to push air down to the sweating family.

My brother said, "I guess we could go get some at a hardware store in town," and dad told him, "It's their fault; they shouldn't have rusted chains to begin with. I'm not paying for that. To hell with them. We paid enough for this condo. Ain't worth it."

The next morning, around nine, we'd all awakened and slurped coffee, suited up, and dragged chairs, umbrellas, floats, coolers, and cheap toys to the beach. We'd paid top dollar for all this beach ware at Bob's Beach World, which we'd seen signs for on the interstate the entire trip down crowded I-95; from the planes above, I'd imagined we look like a trail of ants rushing to a pile of leftovers, hauling off our bucket of shells. One elderly beachcombing couple with weathered skin told me the shells were larger at a secluded beach a few miles away. I thanked them and guess we looked like the tourists, though we'd been converging here once a year for ten years.

My daughter and I left our condo and drove to Publix just a mile or two away. I volunteered for the thirty minutes of freedom. We needed to pick up just a few things: milk; bottled water (because the water from the spigot tasted bad); more sunscreen and block and lotion; some chips and salsa, breakfast bars, deli meat, and a toothbrush. No matter how many lists we made, we missed something.

The grocery store at the beach looked like the one back home, minus beach paraphernalia, the large alcohol section, and all the deputy sheriffs. I asked a clerk if they'd been robbed, and she said, "No, a ten year old girl is missing." "Oh," I said, and she responded, "Probably just wondered off." Her eyes scanned the area, as if there's an abductor lurking around, and I hold my own daughter's hand a little harder, and she said, "Daddy, that hurts." "I'm sorry," I said, loosening my grip.

Items purchased, we head back to the condo complex, hidden behind dunes, bushes, and undergrowth, like the million dollar homes drivers can only see the roofs of lining A1A unless they're walking the beach. I sent my daughter to the beach to rejoin her mother, grandparents, aunts, uncles, and cousins, while I drank margaritas, closed my eyes, and listened to the waves crash on the beach.

After grilling, we all head back to the condo to shower, get ready for bed. Someone watching the local news talked about an abduction at Publix, finding a girl looking askew, violated, in the undergrowth just across the street from the Publix shopping center. By morning, they had taken a man into custody for questioning, a sexual predator on parole and living at the beach in an old mobile home park, across from Publix.

Everyone else had gone to the beach or pool the next morning when my daughter awoke, and after a quick breakfast, I helped her with sunscreen. As she dashed out the door, I told her to come back, and I grabbed my hat, keys, and wallet, and I walked with her, keeping a close watch. The cars, trucks, and SUV's in the parking lot were no longer vacationers from various parts of Florida, Georgia, Tennessee, Alabama, and even Arkansas, but were predators. Even the older couple next door from Atlanta with their young grandson I now saw as predators and holding a young child captive.

The Concert

Students nicely dressed greeted patrons and held open the cavernous medieval doors at the entrance of the chapel. Four students, one male and one female on each side, were dressed in black, the men in tuxedos and black bow ties and the women in black knee length dresses and matching pumps. I took one of the programs and as I entered the chapel, I took a seat on the back row. As the crowd shuffled past and took seats on the oak pews, I noted that the majority of the patrons were students, signing roll sheets for extra credit, and I thought it sad that such a performance wasn't better attended by faculty, staff, and administrators. There were a few community supporters, all elderly, and I imagined free events like these were their life preservers, them clinging to their lives, and to their youth, through students. My own grandmother, taking what would be her last round of chemotherapy (the therapy part didn't seem to match the outcomes) had confided that her mind felt youthful, but her body was somehow incongruent with her mind. She felt like an imposter in her own skin. She'd said, "I look at my feet and don't think they're mine."

As the soprano came forward, she talked of lullabies, but with the lights down, I couldn't read the program. As the piano accompanist softly tapped the keys, the piano player hunched and raised his arms above the keys in dramatic gestures. The soprano's voice reverberated in the chapel, and I closed my eyes remembering lullabies I sang to my children to induce sleep when they were young and recalled the smell of baby powder, the overstuffed yellow rocking chair, and the music mobile playing the same lullaby that hung over the baby bed that seemed to soothe. As the soprano explained before she broke into the lullaby, the story behind the lullaby wasn't as pleasing; there was some indication the history of "The Little Horses" was sung by a slave to white children when she couldn't sing it to her own. I wonder how many songs and rhymes have origins or meanings beyond the surface that we never know or think about, and the first that entered my mind was: "Peter, Peter, pumpkin eater, had a wife and couldn't keep her; put her in a pumpkin shell, and there he kept her very well."

I watched the backs of the college students on the row in front of me, how they were attentive, how some of the males' hair styles were long and unkempt, and I imagined my own probably looked that way in college. I wondered if they enjoyed the faculty music concert, if they were paying attention, if they would ever attend another cultural event. Mostly, I fanned my face with the program. The chapel was hot and stuffy and I hoped no one passed out.

The crowd clapped, and a student brought a chair to the stage and a metal music stand, and once he exited, a saxophone player appeared next to a different piano accompanist, and music that nearly put me to sleep before now set me on edge. I assume the vibrations stirred up a wasp nest on an upper rafter of the triangular wood roof, and the wasps began to move from one side of inset lights in the arched ceiling to the other side. Occasionally, one of them would dip down to the crowd, and I imagined one of the students getting stung and yelling something obscene, stopping the performance cold in its tracks: "Holy shit, I've been stung!" I imagined the few community members calling the president to complain and the dean having to call them one by one to apologize.

The third and final performance was by a part time faculty member who played the Spanish guitar – Capricho Arabe by Francisco Tarrega and Jean-Baptiste Singelee's Fantaisie, Op. 50. While listening to the Spanish guitar is beautiful, I gazed at the triangular pattern in the green and yellow stained glass windows. I shifted from one cheek to another and tried to align my backbone with the pew to alleviate discomfort. I ate a mint and I thought about my day and the next day, and at the end of the Singelee piece, I realized I hadn't heard much at all; still, I clapped with the crowd and wondered if I would follow the crowd in a crime by doing nothing, not paying attention. I figured I might.

As I left the building, buttoning my coat from the freezing cold and wind, I thought about how nice it was for others to see a college employee at the event, but I also thought about how many hours, days, weeks, months pass by when I'm not present, when I'm in the past or the future, trying to grapple with life and all its complexity. I should stop and enjoy the moments because they don't return. I want to look at my feet and know them.

Florida Beware

I slid my credit card twice before it took at the Shell gas pump just off interstate 75 in Southern Georgia, ten miles from the Florida State line. I stretched and looked around the well-lit station and convenience store. It seemed newer and clean, and my wife and kids scurried inside to use the restrooms, since we wouldn't stop again until we got to the 1930's lodge at Wakulla Springs in Northern Florida, the site for scenes from iconic movies such as *Creature from the Black Lagoon, Tarzan's Secret Treasure, Airport 77,* and *Around the World in 80 Days*. The Cypress trees draped in Spanish moss in the clear water and deep caves were still mysterious and not completely understood.

Bordering the Shell station was a make-shift stand with a fellow who sold walking canes, oranges, and boiled peanuts. While I waited on the pump to fill our SUV, a black minivan pulled in on the other side, and a woman wearing black and white leggings that looked like piano keys, a t-shirt I couldn't quite read without my readers, and flip-flops got out, started the pump. She got back in, her minivan door hung open, and she sprawled in the seat texting. She didn't even seem alerted that I was just a few feet away and I hoped my wife was more careful. Sure, I might not *look* threatening, but that wasn't the point.

With the lever set, I moved around the SUV, cleaned the windshield in the front and back and then wiped the mirrors with paper towels. I heard the valve shut off, and when I finished, I walked back around to top the gas off. Before I stopped, I heard a tear and slam and looked over to see the lady taking off through the parking lot in her minivan with the pump nozzle still in the tank, the metal bracket and hose dragging. When it snapped off, the force left a dent in her automatic side door. When she heard the noise, she slammed on brakes, jumped out, pulled the nozzle out of the tank, threw it on the ground, and took off up the ramp toward Florida. I was relieved to learn of safety features to prevent an explosion.

The owner of Indian decent ran from the store yelling, "You bitch. You pay," but bitch came out beach. I heard a lone siren about the time my wife and kids came out of the store and I yelled, "Hurry up." I drove off, the buckle alarm beeping. "What in the world is it?" my wife asked. I told her the story, told her I didn't want to get caught up as a witness, and that the owner had seen as much as me. I wondered if the woman got bad news from a text---maybe a relative or friend died or maybe she was upset with her husband or children or maybe she was distracted by something about her job or maybe she just had dementia like a lot of folks in the retiree state. Could've been anything, but what I was worried about most was that she was on the same interstate as we were headed to Florida and might strike again.

Sanctuary

I zipped my pants, washed my hands, and heard someone yell "Help!" I looked around the restroom, and I heard the voice again: "Help me! They're shooting at me." I peeked out the window and noted a young man waving his arms.

"Help me," he yelled. "They're going to kill me."

I didn't see anyone chasing him, nor had I heard gun fire, and I wondered if he was one of the mentally ill homeless who wandered around town between meals and slept at the shelter. Since I had been on the job with the insurance firm, there had been about three shootings in the neighborhood, and I was always on guard.

I sprinted out of my office and asked the administrative assistant to call the police, but someone already had. Sirens wailed and blue lights flashed in our parking lot and I raised my window to hear once the sirens were off.

I could discern the poor fellow was convinced someone was chasing, shooting at him, and he was looking for sanctuary.

When they asked for his ID, he pulled out his wallet and a plastic sandwich bag of crack cocaine fell out, and he was immediately handcuffed and moved to the backseat of the patrol car. I heard them read the Miranda rights and they asked why he had a bag of crack. He confessed he took it from the dealer and ran without paying and that's why they were chasing and shooting at him. He cried out he didn't want to be shot and die.

Later in the afternoon, a woman who claimed to be the fellow's mother came to our office to complain about us calling the police, as if her son's arrest were somehow our fault. Said she'd change insurance companies. The security guard escorted her outside and they talked briefly, but I couldn't hear.

I felt good the fellow found sanctuary, though not the type for which he'd hoped, and I wanted his circumstances to put him on a new path to conquer addiction and avoid homelessness, but I read in the newspaper later that week they found him hanging in his cell. While the investigation was reported to be ongoing, they suspected suicide, though rumor was the dealer who'd been caught later the same day might have done it for revenge. If it's ruled suicide, since there were no witnesses, no camera, and no evidence, the mother will be back, because the insurance policy won't pay.

About the Author

Niles Reddick's collection Road Kill Art and Other Oddities was a finalist for an Eppie award; his novel Lead Me Home was a national finalist for a ForeWord Award and a finalist in the Georgia Author of the Year award in the fiction category; and his novel Drifting too far from the Shore was a nominee for a Pulitzer Prize and a Pen Faulkner award.

His work has appeared in several anthologies: Southern Voices in Every Direction (Iris Press), Unusual Circumstances (Pocol Press), Getting Old (KY Story Press), Happy Holidays (Kind of Hurricane Press), Dis-or-der (Red Dashboard), Flash! A Collection (The Fictional Café), and in Short Story America.

Author of over hundred short stories published in literary magazines and journals all over the world, Niles and his family make their home in Jackson, Tennessee, where he serves as the Vice Provost for the University of Memphis, Lambuth. His website is http://nilesreddick.com/

Acknowledgements

My sincere appreciation goes to each of the editors who accepted and published versions of my stories in journals all over the world including: "The Last Word" and "Angler's Prayer" in *The Miscreant Magazine*; "The Ministry" in *The Red Dirt Review*, in *In Flight Literary Magazine,* and as a podcast in *No Extra Words*; "The Pool" (a Pushcart nominee) in *The Olive Press;* "Visiting" in *Drunk Monkeys;* "Worm Grunting" (a Best of the Web nominee) in *The Harpoon Review*; "The Logic of High" in *Wordsmith Literary*; "Little Man" in *Sonder Literary Magazine* and as a podcast with Manawaker Studios; "Miracle", "It Will Get Worse", and "Losing My Religion" in *SoFloPoJo* (*South Florida Poetry Journal*); "Reading Coffee Grounds" in *Corner Club Press*; "Birthday Present" in *The OFI Press*; "Checking In" in *Spelk*; "My Rat War" in *The Borfski Press*; "Sex Offender" in *Ham Literature*; "The Tooth" in *The Story Shack*; "Oedipus" and "Looney Tunes" in *The Piker Press*; "Dog War" in *Dead Mule School of Southern Literature*; "The Jog" in *Zero Flash*; "Hokey Pokey" in *Firefly Magazine*; "Mud Island Monorail" in *Southern Reader*; "The Cleaners" in *Flash: The International Short-Short Story Magazine*; "Car Wash" in *Storyland*; "Wet Nurse", "Whistler", and "A Porsche for Me" in *Koru Magazine*; "The Brand" in *NOTLA Digital*; "The Reviewer" in *Carpe Arte Journal*; "Oldies Concert" and "Merger" in *The Basil O'Flaherty Literary Magazine*; "Maxine" in *Former People: Bangs, Whimpers, Arts, Culture and Commentary*; "O Christmas Tree" in *Slice of Life* and in the anthology *Happy Holidays*; "First Pitch" as a podcast in *No Extra Words*; "Heart Attack" in *Like the Dew: A Journal of Southern Culture and Politics*; "History" in *Cicatrix Publishing*; "Staying Close" in *The Gambler*; "Damascus Road" in *Tuck Magazine*, and "The Concert" in *The Faircloth Review*; and "Sanctuary" in *The Schuylkill Valley Journal*.

CPSIA information can be obtained
at www.ICGtesting.com
Printed in the USA
LVHW04s0720070818
586181LV00004B/4/P

9 781938 436505